Alfred, Lord Tennyson

Becket

Alfred, Lord Tennyson

Becket

ISBN/EAN: 9783741192784

Manufactured in Europe, USA, Canada, Australia, Japa

Cover: Foto ©Andreas Hilbeck / pixelio.de

Manufactured and distributed by brebook publishing software
(www.brebook.com)

Alfred, Lord Tennyson

Becket

BECKET · ·

BY

ALFRED, LORD TENNYSON

ILLUSTRATED BY F. C. GORDON

NEW YORK
DODD, MEAD & COMPANY
MDCCCXCIV

THE CAXTON PRESS
NEW YORK

BECKET

TENNYSON

DRAMATIS PERSONÆ.

HENRY II. (*son of the Earl of Anjou*).

THOMAS BECKET, *Chancellor of England, afterwards Archbishop of Canterbury.*

GILBERT FOLIOT, *Bishop of London.*

ROGER, *Archbishop of York.*

Bishop of Hereford.

HILARY, *Bishop of Chichester.*

JOCELYN, *Bishop of Salisbury.*

JOHN OF SALISBURY, } *Friends of Becket.*
HERBERT OF BOSHAM, }

WALTER MAP, *reputed author of "Golias," Latin poems against the priesthood.*

KING LOUIS OF FRANCE.

GEOFFREY, *son of Rosamund and Henry.*

GRIM, *a monk of Cambridge.*

SIR REGINALD FITZURSE, ⎤
SIR RICHARD DE BRITO, ⎟ *the four knights of the King's household,*
SIR WILLIAM DE TRACY, ⎟ *enemies of Becket.*
SIR HUGH DE MORVILLE, ⎦

DE BROC OF SALTWOOD CASTLE.

LORD LEICESTER.

PHILIP DE ELEEMOSYNA.

TWO KNIGHT TEMPLARS.

JOHN OF OXFORD (*called the Swearer*).

ELEANOR OF AQUITAINE, *Queen of England (divorced from Louis of France).*

ROSAMUND DE CLIFFORD.

MARGERY.

Knights, Monks, Beggars, etc.

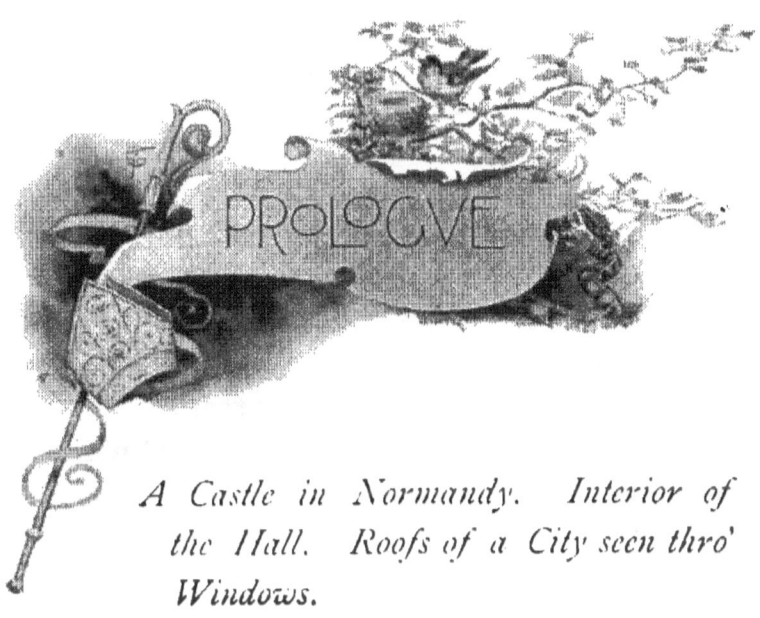

PROLOGVE

A Castle in Normandy. Interior of the Hall. Roofs of a City seen thro' Windows.

HENRY *and* BECKET *at Chess.*

Henry. So then our good Archbishop Theo-
      bald
    Lies dying.
Becket. I am grieved to know as much.
Henry. But we must have a mightier man
    than he
For his successor.
Becket. Have you thought of one?
Henry. A cleric lately poison'd his own
    mother,
And being brought before the courts of the
    Church,

They but degraded him. I hope they whipt him.
I would have hang'd him.

Becket.   It is your move.

Henry.   Well—there.   [*Moves.*

The Church in the pell-mell of Stephen's time
Hath climb'd the throne and almost clutch'd the
          crown ;
But by the royal customs of our realm
The Church should hold her baronies of me,
Like other lords amenable to law.
I'll have them written down and made the law.

Becket. My liege, I move my bishop.

Henry.   And if I live,
No man without my leave shall excommunicate
My tenants or my household.

Becket.   Look to your king.

Henry. No man, without my leave, shall
          cross the seas
To set the Pope against me—I pray your pardon.

Becket. Well—will you move ?

Henry.   There.   [*Moves.*

Becket.   Check—you move so wildly.

Henry. There then !   [*Moves.*

Becket. Why—there then, for you see my
          bishop
Hath brought your king to a standstill. You are
          beaten.

Henry (*kicks over the board*). Why, there
          then—down go bishop and king together.

I loathe being beaten ; had I fixt my fancy
Upon the game I should have beaten thee,
But that was vagabond.

Becket. Where, my liege ? With Phryne,
Or Lais, or thy Rosamund, or another?

Henry. My Rosamund is no Lais, Thomas
Becket ;
And yet she plagues me too—no fault in her—
But that I fear the Queen would have her life.

Becket. Put her away, put her away, my liege !
Put her away into a nunnery !
Safe enough there from her to whom thou art
bound
By Holy Church. And wherefore should she
seek
The life of Rosamund de Clifford more
Than that of other paramours of thine ?

Henry. How dost thou know I am not wedded
to her?

Becket. How should I know ?

Henry. That is my secret, Thomas.

Becket. State secrets should be patent to the
statesman
Who serves and loves his king, and whom the
king
Loves not as statesman, but true lover and
friend.

Henry. Come, come, thou art but deacon, not
yet bishop,

No, nor archbishop, nor my confessor yet.
I would to God thou wert, for I should find
An easy father confessor in thee.
    Becket.   St. Denis, that thou shouldst not. I
       should beat
Thy kingship as my bishop hath beaten it.
    Henry.   Hell take thy bishop then, and my
       kingship too !
Come, come, I love thee and I know thee, I know
       thee,
A doter on white pheasant-flesh at feasts,
A sauce-deviser for thy days of fish,
A dish-designer, and most amorous
Of good old red sound liberal Gascon wine :
Will not thy body rebel, man, if thou flatter it ?
    Becket.   That palate is insane which cannot
       tell
A good dish from a bad, new wine from old.
    Henry.   Well, who loves wine loves woman.
    Becket.   So I do.
Men are God's trees, and women are God's
       flowers ;
And when the Gascon wine mounts to my head,
The trees are all the statelier, and the flowers
Are all the fairer.
    Henry.   And thy thoughts, thy fancies ?
    Becket.   Good dogs, my liege, well train'd,
       and easily called
Off from the game.

Henry. Save for some once or twice,
When they ran down the game and worried it.
    Becket. No, my liege, no!—not once—in
    God's name, no!
    Henry. Nay, then, I take thee at thy word—
    believe thee
The veriest Galahad of old Arthur's hall.
And so this Rosamund, my true heart-wife,
Not Eleanor—she whom I love indeed
As a woman should be loved—Why dost thou
    smile
So dolorously?
    Becket. My good liege, if a man
Wastes himself among women, how should he
    love
A woman, as a woman should be loved?
    Henry. How shouldst thou know that never
    hast loved one?
Come, I would give her to thy care in England
When I am out in Normandy or Anjou.
    Becket. My lord, I am your subject, not your—
    Henry. Pander.
God's eyes! I know all that—not my purveyor
Of pleasures, but to save a life—her life;
Ay, and the soul of Eleanor from hell-fire.
I have built a secret bower in England, Thomas,
A nest in a bush.
    Becket. And where, my liege?
    Henry (whispers). Thine ear.

Becket.   That's lone enough.

Henry (laying paper on table). This chart here
    mark'd " *Her Bower*,"
Take, keep it, friend.   See, first, a circling wood,
A hundred pathways running every way,
And then a brook, a bridge ; and after that
This labyrinthine brickwork maze in maze,
And then another wood, and in the midst
A garden and my Rosamund.   Look, this line—
The rest you see is color'd green,—but this
Draws thro' the chart to her.

Becket.   This blood-red line ?

Henry.   Ay ! blood, perchance, except thou
    see to her.

Becket.   And where is, she ?   There in her
    English nest ?

Henry.   Would God she were—no, here within
    the city.
We take her from her secret bower in Anjou
And pass her to her secret bower in England.
She is ignorant of all but that I love her.

Becket.   My liege, I pray thee let me hence : a
    widow
And orphan child, whom   one   of   thy   wild
    barons—

Henry.   Ay, ay, but swear to see to her in Eng-
    land.

Becket.   Well, well, I swear, but not to please
    myself.

Henry. Whatever come between us?

Becket.   What should come
Between us, Henry?

Henry.   Nay—I know not, Thomas.

Becket. What need then? Well—whatever
come between us.   [*Going.*

Henry. A moment! thou didst help me to
my throne
In Theobald's time, and after by thy wisdom
Hast kept it firm from shaking; but now I,
For my realm's sake, myself must be the wizard
To raise that tempest which will set it trembling
Only to base it deeper. I, true son
Of Holy Church—no croucher to the Gregories
That tread the kings their children underheel—
Must curb her; and the Holy Father, while
This Barbarossa butts him from his chair,
Will need my help—be facile to my hands.
Now is my time. Yet—lest there should be
flashes
And fulminations from the side of Rome,
An interdict on England—I will have
My young son Henry crown'd the King of Eng-
land,
That so the Papal bolt may pass by England,
As seeming his, not mine, and fall abroad.
I'll have it done—and now.

Becket.   Surely too young
Even for this shadow of a crown; and tho'

I love him heartily, I can spy already
A strain of hard and headstrong in him.   Say,
The   Queen   should   play   his   kingship   against
    thine !
    Henry.   I will not think so, Thomas.   Who
    shall crown him ?
Canterbury is dying.
    Becket.   The next Canterbury.
    Henry.   And   who   shall   he   be,   my   friend
    Thomas ?   Who ?
    Becket.   Name him ; the Holy Father will con-
    firm him.
    Henry (*lays his hand on Becket's shoulder*).
    Here !
    Becket.   Mock   me   not.   I am   not   even   a
    monk.
Thy   jest—no   more.   Why—look—is   this   a
    sleeve
For an archbishop ?
    Henry.   But the   arm within
Is Becket's, who hath beaten down my foes.
    Becket.   A soldier's, not a spiritual arm.
    Henry.   I lack a spiritual soldier, Thomas—
A man of this world and the next to boot.
    Becket.   There's Gilbert Foliot.
    Henry.   He ! too thin, too thin.
Thou art the man to fill out the Church robe ;
Your Foliot fasts and fawns too much for me.
    Becket.   Roger of York.

Henry.   Roger is Roger of York.
King, Church, and State to him but foils wherein
To set that precious jewel, Roger of York.
No.
  Becket.   Henry of Winchester?
  Henry.   Him who crown'd Stephen—
King Stephen's brother! No; too royal for me.
And I'll have no more Anselms.
  Becket.   Sire, the business
Of thy whole kingdom waits me : let me go.
  Henry.   Answer me first.
  Becket.   Then for thy barren jest
Take thou mine answer in bare commonplace—
Nolo episcopari.
  Henry.   Ay, but *Nolo*
Archiepiscopari, my good friend,
Is quite another matter.
  Becket.   A more awful one.
Make *me* archbishop! Why, my liege, I know
Some three or four poor priests a thousand times
Fitter for this grand function. *Me* archbishop!
God's favor and king's favor might so clash
That thou and I—That were a jest indeed!
  Henry.   Thou angerest me, man : I do not jest.

Enter ELEANOR *and* SIR REGINALD FITZURSE.

Eleanor (singing).

>   Over! the sweet summer closes,
>   The reign of the roses is done—

Henry (to Becket, who is going). Thou shalt
not go. I have not ended with thee.

Eleanor (seeing chart on table). This chart
with the red line! her bower! whose bower?

Henry. The chart is not mine, but Becket's:
take it, Thomas.

Eleanor. Becket! O—ay—and these chess-
men on the floor—the king's crown broken!
Becket hath beaten thee again—and thou hast
kicked down the board. I know thee of old.

Henry. True enough, my mind was set upon
other matters.

Eleanor. What matters? State matters?
love matters?

Henry. My love for thee, and thine for me.

Eleanor.

> Over! the sweet summer closes,
>   The reign of the roses is done;
> Over and gone with the roses,
>   And over and gone with the sun.

Here; but our sun in Aquitaine lasts longer.
I would I were in Aquitaine again—your north
chills me.

> Over! the sweet summer closes,
>   And never a flower at the close:
> Over and gone with the roses,
>   And winter again and the snows.

That was not the way I ended it first—but un-
symmetrically, preposterously, illogically, out of

passion, without art—like a song of the people.
Will you have it? The last Parthian shaft of a
forlorn Cupid at the King's left breast, and all
left-handedness and under-handedness.

> And never a flower at the close,
> Over and gone with the roses,
> Not over and gone with the rose.

True, one rose will outblossom the rest, one rose
in a bower. I speak after my fancies, for I am a
Troubadour, you know, and won the violet at
Toulouse; but my voice is harsh here, not in
tune, a nightingale out of season; for marriage,
rose or no rose, has killed the golden violet.

Becket. Madam, you do ill to scorn wedded
love.

Eleanor. So I do. Louis of France loved me,
and I dreamed that I loved Louis of France; and
I loved Henry of England, and Henry of England
dreamed that he loved me; but the marriage-
garland withers even with the putting on, the
bright link rusts with the breath of the first after-
marriage kiss, the harvest moon is the ripening
of the harvest, and the honeymoon is the gall of
love; he dies of his honeymoon. I could pity
this poor world myself that it is no better ordered.

Henry. Dead is he, my Queen? What, altogether? Let me swear nay to that by this
cross on thy neck. God's eyes! what a lovely
cross! what jewels!

Eleanor. Doth it please you? Take it and wear it on that hard heart of yours—there.

[*Gives it to him.*

Henry (*puts it on*). On this left breast before
  so hard a heart,
To hide the scar left by thy Parthian dart.

Eleanor. Has my simple song set you jingling? Nay, if I took and translated that hard heart into our Provençal facilities, I could so play about it with the rhyme—

Henry. That the heart were lost in the rhyme and the matter in the metre. May we not pray you, Madam, to spare us the hardness of your facility?

Eleanor. The wells of Castaly are not wasted upon the desert. We did but jest.

Henry. There's no jest on the brows of Herbert there. What is it, Herbert?

Enter HERBERT OF BOSHAM.

Herbert. My liege, the good Archbishop is no more.

Henry. Peace to his soul!

Herbert. I left him with peace on his face— that sweet other-world smile, which will be reflected in the spiritual body among the angels. But he longed much to see your Grace and the Chancellor ere he past, and his last words were a commendation of Thomas Becket to your Grace as his successor in the archbishopric.

Henry. Ha, Becket! thou rememberest our talk?

Becket. My heart is full of tears—I have no answer.

Henry. Well, well, old men must die, or the world would grow mouldy, would only breed the past again. Come to me to-morrow. Thou hast but to hold out thy hand. Meanwhile the revenues are mine. A-hawking, a-hawking! If I sit, I grow fat. [*Leaps over the table, and exit.*

Becket. He did prefer me to the chancellorship.
Believing I should ever aid the Church—
But have I done it? He commends me now
From out his grave to this archbishopric.

Herbert. A dead man's dying wish should be
    of weight.

Becket. His should. Come with me. Let me
    learn at full
The manner of his death, and all he said.
                [*Exeunt* HERBERT *and* BECKET.

Eleanor.   Fitzurse, that chart with the red line
—thou sawest it—her bower.

Fitzurse.   Rosamund's ?

Eleanor.   Ay—there lies the secret of her
whereabouts, and the King gave it to his Chancellor.

Fitzurse.   To this son of a London merchant—
how your Grace must hate him.

Eleanor.   Hate him? as brave a soldier as
Henry and a goodlier man : but thou—dost thou
love this Chancellor, that thou hast sworn a volun-
tary allegiance to him ?

Fitzurse.   Not for my love toward him, but
because he had the love of the King.   How
should a baron love a beggar on horseback, with
the retinue of three kings behind him, outroyal-
ling royalty?   Besides, he holp the King to
break down our castles, for the which I hate
him.

Eleanor.   For the which I honor him.   Statesman not Churchman he.   A great and sound
policy that : I could embrace him for it : you
could not see the King for the kinglings.

Fitzurse.   Ay, but he speaks to a noble as
tho' he were a churl, and to a churl as if he were
a noble.

Eleanor.   Pride of the plebeian !

Fitzurse.   And this plebeian like to be Archbishop !

Eleanor. True, and I have an inherited loathing of these black sheep of the Papacy. Archbishop? I can see further into a man than our hot-headed Henry, and if there ever come feud between Church and Crown, and I do not then charm this secret out of our loyal Thomas, I am not Eleanor.

Fitzurse. Last night I followed a woman in the city here. Her face was veiled, but the back methought was Rosamund—his paramour, thy rival. I can feel for thee.

Eleanor. Thou feel for me!—paramour—rival! King Louis had no paramours, and I loved him none the more. Henry had many, and I loved him none the less—now neither more nor less—not at all ; the cup's empty. I would she were but his paramour, for men tire of their fancies ; but I fear this one fancy hath taken root, and borne blossom too, and she, whom the King loves indeed, is a power in the State. Rival !— ay, and when the King passes, there may come a crash and embroilment as in Stephen's time ; and her children—canst thou not—that secret matter which would heat the King against thee (*whispers him and he starts*). Nay, that is safe with me as with thyself: but canst thou not—thou art drowned in debt—thou shalt have our love, our silence, and our gold—canst thou not—if thou light upon her—free me from her ?

Fitzurse. Well, Madam, I have loved her in my time.

Eleanor. No, my dear, thou hast not. My Courts of Love would have held thee guiltless of love—the fine attractions and repulses, the delicacies, the subtleties.

Fitzurse. Madam, I loved according to the main purpose and intent of nature.

Eleanor. I warrant thee! thou wouldst hug thy Cupid till his ribs cracked—enough of this. Follow me this Rosamund day and night, whithersoever she goes; track her, if thou canst, even into the King's lodging, that I may (*clenches her fist*)—may at least have my cry against him and her,—and thou in thy way shouldst be jealous of the King, for thou in thy way didst once, what shall I call it, affect her thine own self.

Fitzurse. Ay, but the young colt winced and whinnied and flung up her heels; and then the King came honeying about her, and this Becket, her father's friend, like enough staved us from her.

Eleanor. Us!

Fitzurse. Yes, by the Blessed Virgin! There were more than I buzzing round the blossom— De Tracy—even that flint De Brito.

Eleanor. Carry her off among you; run in upon her and devour her, one and all of you; make her as hateful to herself and to the King, as she is to me.

Fitzurse. I and all would be glad to wreak our spite on the rosefaced minion of the King, and bring her to the level of the dust, so that the King—

Eleanor. Let her eat it like the serpent, and be driven out of her paradise.

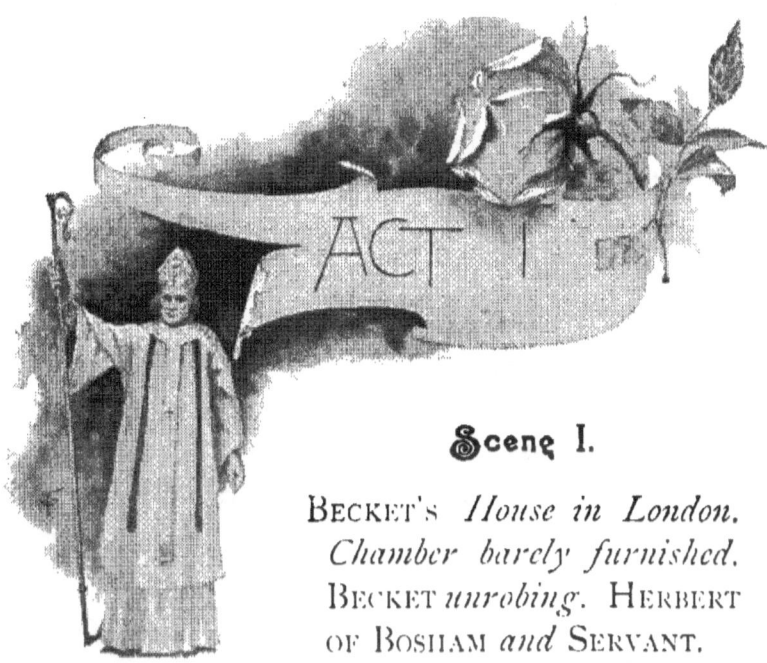

ACT I

Scene I.

BECKET's *House in London.*
Chamber barely furnished.
BECKET *unrobing.* HERBERT
OF BOSHAM *and* SERVANT.

Servant. Shall I not help your lordship to
your rest?
Becket. Friend, am I so much better than thy-
self
That thou shouldst help me? Thou art wearied
out
With this day's work, get thee to thine own
bed.
Leave me with Herbert, friend. [*Exit* SERVANT.
Help me off, Herbert, with this—and this.
Herbert. Was not the people's blessing as
we past
Heart-comfort and a balsam to thy blood?

27

Becket.   The people know their Church a
  tower of strength,
A bulwark against Throne and Baronage.
Too heavy for me, this; off with it, Her-
  bert!
  Herbert.   Is it so much heavier than thy Chan-
  cellor's robe?
  Becket.   No; but the Chancellor's and the
  Archbishop's
Together more than mortal man can bear.
  Herbert.   Not heavier than thine armor at
  Toulouse?
  Becket.   O Herbert, Herbert, in my chancellor-
  ship
I more than once have gone against the
  Church.
  Herbert.   To please the King?
  Becket.   Ay, and the King of kings,
Or justice; for it seem'd to me but just
The Church should pay her scutage like the
  lords.
But hast thou heard this cry of Gilbert Foliot
That I am not the man to be your Primate,
For Henry could not work a miracle—
Make an Archbishop of a soldier?
  Herbert.   Ay,
For Gilbert Foliot held himself the man.
  Becket.   Am I the man?   My mother, ere she
  bore me,

Dream'd that twelve stars fell glittering out of
    heaven
Into her bosom.
    Herbert.   Ay, the fire, the light,
The spirit of the twelve Apostles enter'd
Into thy making.
    Becket.   And when I was a child,
The Virgin, in a vision of my sleep,
Gave me the golden keys of Paradise.   Dream,
Or prophecy, that?
    Herbert.   Well, dream and prophecy
    both.
    Becket. And when I was of Theobald's house-
    hold, once—
The good old man would sometimes have his
    jest—
He took his mitre off, and set it on me,
And said, " My young Archbishop—thou wouldst
    make
A stately Archbishop ! "   Jest or prophecy
    there ?
    Herbert. Both, Thomas, both.
    Becket.   Am I the man ?   That rang
Within my head last night, and when I slept
Methought I stood in Canterbury Minster,
And spake to the Lord God, and said, " O
    Lord,
I have been a lover of wines, and delicate
    meats,

And secular splendors, and a favorer
Of players, and a courtier, and a feeder
Of dogs and hawks, and apes, and lions, and
    lynxes.
Am *I* the man?" And the Lord answer'd
    me,
"Thou art the man, and all the more the
    man."
And then I asked again, "O Lord my
    God,
Henry the King hath been my friend, my
    brother,
And mine uplifter in this world, and chosen
    me
For this Thy great archbishopric, believing
That I should go against the Church with
    him,
And I shall go against him with the Church,
And I have said no word of this to him :
Am *I* the man?" And the Lord answer'd
    me,
"Thou art the man, and all the more the
    man."
And thereupon, methought, He drew toward
    me,
And smote me down upon the Minster floor.
I fell.
    Herbert. God make not thee, but thy foes,.
    fall.

Becket. I fell. Why fall? Why did He smite
  me? What?
Shall I fall off—to please the King once more?
Not fight—tho' somehow traitor to the King—
My truest and mine utmost for the Church?
  Herbert. Thou canst not fall that way. Let
    traitor be;
For how have fought thine utmost for the
    Church,
Save from the throne of thine archbishopric?
And how been made Archbishop hadst thou told
    him,
"I mean to fight mine utmost for the Church,
Against the King?"
  Becket. But dost thou think the King
Forced mine election?
  Herbert. I do think the King
Was potent in the election, and why not?
Why should not Heaven have so inspired the
    King?
Be comforted. Thou art the man—be thou
A mightier Anselm.
  Becket. I do believe thee, then. I am the
    man.
And yet I seem appall'd—on such a sudden
At such an eagle-height I stand and see
The rift that runs between me and the King.
I served our Theobald well when I was with
    him;

I served King Henry well as Chancellor;
I am his no more, and I must serve the
    Church.
This Canterbury is only less than Rome,
And all my doubts I fling from me like
    dust,
Winnow and scatter all scruples to the wind,
And all the puissance of the warrior,
And all the wisdom of the Chancellor,
And all the heap'd experiences of life,
I cast upon the side of Canterbury—
Our holy mother Canterbury, who sits
With tatter'd robes.   Laics and barons, thro'
The random gifts of careless kings, have
    graspt
Her livings, her advowsons, granges, farms,
And goodly acres—we will make her whole ;
Not one rood lost.   And for these royal
    customs,
These ancient royal customs,—they *are* Royal,
Not of the Church—and let them be anathema,
And all that speak for them anathema.
    Herbert.   Thomas, thou art moved too much.
    Becket.   O Herbert, here
I gash myself asunder from the King,
Tho' leaving each, a wound ; mine own, a
    grief
To show the scar forever—his, a hate
Not ever to be heal'd.

Enter Rosamund de Clifford, *flying from* Sir
    Reginald Fitzurse.   *Drops her veil.*

Becket.   Rosamund de Clifford!

Rosamund.   Save me, father, hide me—they
follow me—and I must not be known.
Becket.   Pass in with Herbert there.
                 [*Exeunt* Rosamund *and* Herbert
                 by side door.

Enter FITZURSE.

Fitzurse.   The Archbishop!

Becket.   Ay! what wouldst thou, Reginald?

Fitzurse.   Why—why, my lord, I follow'd—
   follow'd one—

Becket.   And then what follows?   Let me
   follow thee.

Fitzurse.   It much imports me I should know
   her name.

Becket.   What her?

Fitzurse.   The woman that I follow'd hither.

Becket.   Perhaps it may import her all as much
Not to be known.

Fitzurse.   And what care I for that?
Come, come, my lord Archbishop; I saw that
   door   .
Close even now upon the woman.

Becket.   Well?

Fitzurse (*making for the door*).   Nay, let me
   pass, my lord, for I must know.

Becket.   Back, man!

Fitzurse.   Then tell me who and what she is.

Becket.   Art thou so sure thou followedst any-
   thing?
Go home, and sleep thy wine off, for thine eyes
Glare stupid-wild with wine.

Fitzurse (*making to the door*).   I must and will.
I care not for thy new archbishopric.

Becket. Back, man, I tell thee ! What !
Shall I forget my new archbishopric
And smite thee with my crozier on the skull ?
'Fore God, I am a mightier man than thou.
 Fitzurse. It well befits thy new archbishopric
To take the vagabond woman of the street
Into thine arms !
 Becket.   O drunken ribaldry !
Out, beast ! out, bear !
 Fitzurse.   I shall remember this.
 Becket. Do, and begone ! [*Exit* FITZURSE.
  (*Going to the door, sees* DE TRACY.)
       Tracy, what dost thou here ?
 De Tracy. My lord, I follow'd Reginald
  Fitzurse.
 Becket. Follow him out !
 De Tracy.   I shall remember this
Discourtesy.   [*Exit.*
 Becket. Do. These be those baron-brutes
That havock'd all the land in Stephen's day.
Rosamund de Clifford.

   Reënter ROSAMUND *and* HERBERT.

 Rosamund.   Here am I.
 Becket.   Why here ?
We gave thee to the charge of John of Salisbury,
To pass thee to thy secret bower to-morrow.
Wast thou not told to keep thyself from sight ?

Rosamund.   Poor bird of passage! so I was ;
    but, father,
They say that you are wise in winged things,
And know the ways of Nature.   Bar the
    bird
From following the fled summer—a chink—he's
    out,
Gone !   And there stole into the city a breath
Full of the meadows, and it minded me
Of the sweet woods of Clifford, and the walks
Where I could move at pleasure, and I thought
Lo ! I must out or die.
    Becket.   Or out *and* die.
And what hast thou to do with this Fitzurse ?
    Rosamund.   Nothing.   He sued my hand.   I
    shook at him.
He found me once alone.—Nay—nay—I cannot
Tell you : my father drove him and his friends,
De Tracy and De Brito, from our castle.
I was but fourteen and an April then.
I heard him swear revenge.
    Becket.   Why will you court it
By self-exposure ? flutter out at night ?
Make it so hard to save a moth from the
    fire ?
    Rosamund.   I have saved many of 'em.   You
    catch 'em, so,
Softly, and fling them out to the free air.
They burn themselves *within*-door.

Becket. Our good John
Must speed you to your bower at once. The
    child
Is there already.
    Rosamund. Yes—the child—the child—
O rare, a whole long day of open field.
    Becket. Ay, but you go disguised.
    Rosamund. O rare again!
We'll baffle them, I warrant. What shall it be?
I'll go as a nun.
    Becket. No.
    Rosamund, What, not good enough
Even to play at nun?
    Becket. Dan John with a nun,
That Map, and these new railers at the Church
May plaister his clean name with scurrilous
    rhymes!
No!
Go like a monk, cowling and clouding up
That fatal star, thy Beauty, from the squint
Of lust and glare of malice. Good night! good
    night!
    Rosamund. Father, I am so tender to all hard-
    ness!
Nay, father, first thy blessing.
    Becket. Wedded?
    Rosamund. Father!
    Becket. Well, well! I ask no more. Heaven
    bless thee! hence!

Rosamund.   O, holy father, when thou seest him
       next,
Commend me to thy friend.
  Becket.   What friend?
  Rosamund.   The King.
  Becket.   Herbert, take out a score of armed
       men
To guard this bird of passage to her cage ;
And watch Fitzurse, and if he follow thee,
Make him thy prisoner.   I am Chancellor yet.
                    [*Exeunt* HERBERT *and* ROSAMUND.
Poor soul ! poor soul !
My friend, the King ! . . . O thou Great Seal of
       England,
Given me by my dear friend the King of Eng-
       land—
We long have wrought together, thou and I—
Now must I send thee as a common friend
To tell the King, my friend, I am against him.
. We are friends no more : he will say that, not I.
The worldly bond between us is dissolved,
Not yet the love : can I be under him
As Chancellor ? as Archbishop over him ?
Go therefore like a friend slighted by one
That hath climb'd up to nobler company.
Not slighted—all but moan'd for : thou must
       go.
I have not dishonor'd thee—I trust I have
       not ;

Not mangled justice. May the hand that
      next
Inherits thee be but as true to thee
As mine hath been! O, my dear friend, the
      King!
O brother!—I may come to martyrdom.
I am martyr in myself already.—Herbert!
   Herbert (reëntering). My lord, the town is
      quiet, and the moon
Divides the whole long street with light and
      shade.
No footfall—no Fitzurse. We have seen her
      home,
   Becket. The hog hath tumbled himself into
      some corner,
Some ditch, to snore away his drunkenness
Into the sober headache,—Nature's moral
Against excess. Let the Great Seal be sent
Back to the King to-morrow.
   Herbert.   Must that be?
The King may rend the bearer limb from limb.
Think on it again.
   Becket.   Against the moral excess
No physical ache, but failure it may be
Of all we aim'd at. John of Salisbury
Hath often laid a cold hand on my heats,
And Herbert hath rebuked me even now.
I will be wise and wary, not the soldier
As Foliot swears it.—John, and out of breath!

Enter JOHN OF SALISBURY.

John of Salisbury.   Thomas, thou wast not
        happy taking charge
Of this wild Rosamund to please the King,
Nor am I happy having charge of her—
The included Danaë has escaped again
Her tower, and her Acrisius—where to seek?
I have been about the city.
    Becket.   Thou wilt find her
Back in her lodging.   Go with her—at once—
To-night—my men will guard you to the gates.
Be sweet to her, she has many enemies.
Send the Great Seal by daybreak.   Both, good-
        night!

Scene II.

Street in Northampton, leading to the Castle.
ELEANOR'S RETAINERS *and* BECKET'S RETAINERS
fighting. Enter ELEANOR *and* BECKET *from opposite streets.*

Eleanor.   Peace, fools !
    Becket.   Peace, friends ! what idle brawl
        is this ?
Retainer of Becket.   They said—her Grace's
    people—thou wast found—
Liars ! I shame to quote 'em—caught, my lord,
With a wanton in thy lodging—Hell requite
    'em !
Retainer of Eleanor.   My liege, the Lord
    Fitzurse reported this
In passing to the Castle even now.
    Retainer of Becket.   And then they mock'd us
    and we fell upon 'em,
For we would live and die for thee, my lord,
However kings and queens may frown on thee.
    Becket (*to his* RETAINERS).   Go, go—no more of
    this !
    Eleanor (*to her* RETAINERS).   Away !—
                [*Exeunt* RETAINERS.
                Fitzurse—

Becket.   Nay, let him be.

Eleanor.   No, no, my Lord Archbishop,
'Tis known you are midwinter to all women,
But often in your chancellorship you served
The follies of the King.

Becket.   No, not these follies !

Eleanor.   My lord, Fitzurse beheld her in your
         lodging.

Becket.   Whom ?

Eleanor.   Well—you know—the min-
         ion, Rosamund.

Becket.   He had good eyes !

Eleanor.   Then, hidden in the street,
He watch'd her pass with John of Salisbury
And heard her cry "Where is this bower of
         mine ? "

Becket.   Good ears too !

Eleanor.   You are going to the Castle,
Will you subscribe the customs ?

Becket.   I leave that,
Knowing how much you reverence Holy Church,
My liege, to your conjecture.

Eleanor.   I and mine—
And many a baron holds along with me—
Are not so much at feud with Holy Church
But we   might   take   your   side   against   the
         customs—
So that you grant me one slight favor.

Becket.   What ?

Eleanor. A sight of that same chart which
    Henry gave you
With the red line—"her bower."
    Becket.   And to what end?
    Eleanor.   That Church must scorn herself
    whose fearful Priest
Sits winking at the license of a king,
Altho' we grant when kings are dangerous
The Church must play into the hands of kings;
Look! I would move this wanton from his sight
And take the Church's danger on myself.
    Becket.   For which she should be duly grate-
    ful.
    Eleanor.   True!
Tho' she that binds the bond, herself should see
That kings are faithful to their marriage vow.
    Becket.   Ay, Madam, and queens also.
    Eleanor.   And queens also!
What is your drift?
    Becket.   My drift is to the Castle,
Where I shall meet the Barons and my King.
                        [*Exit.*

DE BROC, DE TRACY, DE BRITO, DE MORVILLE
               (*passing*).

    Eleanor.   To the Castle?
    De Broc.   Ay!
    Eleanor.   Stir up the King, the Lords!
Set all on fire against him!

De Brito.   Ay, good Madam !
                                   [*Exeunt.*
  Eleanor.   Fool ! I will make thee hateful to
        thy King.
Churl ! I will have thee frightened into France,
And I shall live to trample on thy grave.

Scene III.

The Hall in Northampton Castle.

On one side of the stage the doors of an inner Council-chamber, half open. At the bottom, the great doors of the Hall. ROGER ARCHBISHOP OF YORK, FOLIOT BISHOP OF LONDON, HILARY OF CHICHESTER, BISHOP OF HEREFORD, RICHARD DE HASTINGS (*Grand Prior of Templars*), PHILIP DE ELEEMOSYNA (*the Pope's Almoner*), *and others.* DE BROC, FITZURSE, DE BRITO, DE MORVILLE, DE TRACY, *and other* BARONS *assembled—a table before them.* JOHN OF OXFORD, *President of the Council.*

Enter BECKET *and* HERBERT OF BOSHAM.

Becket.   Where is the King?
       Roger of York.   Gone hawking
            on the Nene,
His heart so gall'd with thine ingratitude,
He will not see thy face till thou hast sign'd
These ancient laws and customs of the realm.
Thy sending back the Great Seal madden'd him,
He all but pluck'd the bearer's eyes away.
Take heed, lest he destroy thee utterly.
   Becket.   Then shalt thou step into my place
       and sign.

Roger of York. Didst thou not promise Henry
  to obey
These ancient laws and customs of the realm?
 Becket. Saving the honor of my order—ay.
Customs, traditions,—clouds that come and go ;
The customs of the Church are Peter's rock.
 Roger of York. Saving thine order ! But
  King Henry sware
That, saving his King's kingship he would grant
  thee
The crown itself. Saving thine order, Thomas,
Is black and white at once, and comes to
  nought.
O bolster'd up with stubbornness and pride,
Wilt thou destroy the Church in fighting for it.
And bring us all to shame?
 Becket.   Roger of York,
When I and thou were youths in Theobald's
  house,
Twice did thy malice and thy calumnies
Exile me from the face of Theobald.
Now I am Canterbury and thou art York.
 Roger of York. And is not York the peer of
  Canterbury?
Did not Great Gregory bid St. Austin here
Found two archbishoprics, London and York?
 Becket. What came of that? The first arch-
  bishop fled,
And York lay barren for a hundred years.

Why, by this rule, Foliot may claim the pall
For London too.
  Foliot.   And with good reason too,
For London had a temple and a priest
When Canterbury hardly bore a name.
  Becket. The pagan temple of a pagan Rome!
The heathen priesthood of a heathen creed!
Thou goest beyond thyself in petulancy!
Who made thee London? Who, but Canter-
   bury?
  John of Oxford. Peace, peace, my lords,
   these customs are no longer
As Canterbury calls them, wandering clouds,
But by the King's command are written down,
And by the King's command, I, John of Oxford,
The President of this Council, read them.
  Becket. Read!
  John of Oxford (reads). "All causes of ad-
vowsons and presentations, whether between
laymen or clerics, shall be tried in the King's
court."
  Becket. But that I cannot sign : for that would
   drag
The cleric before the civil judgment-seat,
And on a matter wholly spiritual.
  John of Oxford. "If any cleric be accused of
felony, the Church shall not protect him ; but he
shall answer to the summons of the King's court
to be tried therein."

Becket.   And that I cannot sign.
Is not the Church the visible Lord on earth?
Shall hands that do create the Lord be bound
Behind the back like laymen-criminals?
The Lord be judged again by Pilate?   No!
   John of Oxford.   "When a bishopric falls
vacant, the King, till another be appointed, shall
receive the revenues thereof."
   Becket.   And that I cannot sign.   Is the King's
      treasury
A fit place for the moneys of the Church,
That be the patrimony of the poor?
   John of Oxford.   "And when the vacancy is
to be filled up, the King shall summon the
chapter of that church to court, and the election
shall be made in the Chapel Royal, with the
consent of our lord the King, and by the advice
of his Government."
   Becket.   And that I cannot sign : for that would
      make
Our island-Church a schism from Christendom,
And weight down all free choice beneath the
      throne.
   Foliot.   And was thine own election so canonical,
Good father?
   Becket.   If it were not, Gilbert Foliot,
I mean to cross the sea to France and lay
My crozier in the Holy Father's hands,
And bid him recreate me, Gilbert Foliot.

Foliot. Nay; by another of these customs
    thou
Wilt not be suffer'd so to cross the seas
Without the license of our lord the King.

Becket. That, too, I cannot sign.

*De Broc, De Brito, De Tracy, Fitzurse, De
    Morville, start up—a clash of swords.*
                    Sign and obey!

Becket. My lords, is this a combat or a council?
Are ye my masters, or my lord the King?
Ye make this clashing for no love o' the customs
Or constitutions, or whate'er ye call them,
But that there be among you those that hold
Lands reft from Canterbury.

De Broc.   And mean to keep them,
In spite of thee!

Lords (shouting). Sign, and obey the crown!

Becket. The crown? Shall I do less for Can-
    terbury
Than Henry for the crown? King Stephen gave
Many of the crown lands to those that helpt him;
So did Matilda, the King's mother. Mark,
When Henry came into his own again,
Then he took back not only Stephen's gifts,
But his own mother's, lest the crown should be
Shorn of ancestral splendor. This did Henry.
Shall I do less for mine own Canterbury?
And thou, De Broc, that holdest Saltwood
    Castle—

De Broc. And mean to hold it, or—
Becket. To have my life.
De Broc. The King is quick to anger ; if thou
    anger him,
We wait but the King's word to strike thee dead.
    Becket. Strike, and I die the death of martyr-
    dom ;
Strike, and ye set these customs by my death
Ringing their own death-knell thro' all the realm.
    Herbert. And I can tell you, lords, ye are all
    as like
To lodge a fear in Thomas Becket's heart
As find a hare's form in a lion's cave.
    John of Oxford. Ay, sheathe your swords, ye
    will displease the King.
    De Broc. Why down then thou ! but an he
    come to Saltwood,
By God's death, thou shalt stick him like a calf !
              [*Sheathing his sword.*
    Hilary. O my good lord, I do entreat thee—
    sign.
Save the King's honor here before his barons.
He hath sworn that thou shouldst sign, and now
    but shuns
The semblance of defeat ; I have heard him say
He means no more ; so if thou sign, my lord,
That were but as the shadow of an assent.
    Becket. 'T would seem too like the substance,
    if I sign'd.

Philip de Eleemosyna. My lord, thine ear! I
    have the ear of the Pope.
As thou hast honor for the Pope our master,
Have pity on him, sorely prest upon
By the fierce Emperor and his Antipope.
Thou knowest he was forced to fly to France;
He pray'd me to pray thee to pacify
Thy King; for if thou go against thy King,
Then must he likewise go against thy King,
And then thy King might join the Antipope,
And that would shake the Papacy as it stands.
Besides, thy King swore to our cardinals
He meant no harm nor damage to the Church.
Smooth thou his pride—thy signing is but form;
Nay, and should harm come of it, it is the
    Pope
Will be to blame—not thou. Over and over
He told me thou shouldst pacify the King,
Lest there be battle between Heaven and Earth,
And Earth should get the better—for the time.
Cannot the Pope absolve thee if thou sign?
    Becket. Have I the orders of the Holy
    Father?
    Philip de Eleemosyna. Orders, my lord—why,
    no; for what am I?
The secret whisper of the Holy Father.
Thou, that hast been a statesman, couldst thou
    always
Blurt thy free mind to the air?

Becket. If Rome be feeble, then should I be
   firm.
Philip. Take it not that way—balk not the
   Pope's will.
When he hath shaken off the Emperor,
He heads the Church against the King with
   thee.
   Richard de Hastings (kneeling). Becket, I am
   the oldest of the Templars ;
I knew thy father ; he would be mine age
Had he lived now ; think of me as thy father !
Behold thy father kneeling to thee, Becket.
Submit ; I promise thee on my salvation
That thou wilt hear no more o' the customs.
   Becket.   What !
Hath Henry told thee ? hast thou talk'd with
   him ?
   Another Templar (kneeling). Father, I am the
   youngest of the Templars,
Look on me as I were thy bodily son,
For, like a son, I lift my hands to thee.
   Philip. Wilt thou hold out for ever, Thomas
   Becket ?
Dost thou not hear ?
   Becket (signs). Why—there then—there—I
   sign,
And swear to obey the customs.
   Foliot.   Is it thy will,
My lord Archbishop, that we too should sign ?

Becket. O ay, by that canonical obedience
Thou still hast owed thy father, Gilbert Foliot.

 Foliot. Loyally and with good faith, my lord
  Archbishop?

 Becket. O ay, with all that loyalty and good
  faith
Thou still hast shown thy primate, Gilbert Foliot.
    [BECKET *draws apart with* HERBERT.
Herbert, Herbert, have I betray'd the Church?
I'll have the paper back—blot out my name.

 Herbert. Too late, my lord: you see they are
  signing there.

 Becket. False to myself—it is the will of
  God
To break me, prove me nothing of myself!
This Almoner hath tasted Henry's gold.
The cardinals have finger'd Henry's gold.
And Rome is venal ev'n to rottenness.
I see it, I see it.
I am no soldier, as he said—at least
No leader. Herbert, till I hear from the Pope
I will suspend myself from all my functions.
If fast and prayer, the lacerating scourge—

 Foliot (*from the table*). My lord Archbishop,
  thou hast yet to seal.

 Becket. First, Foliot, let me see what I have
  sign'd.   [*Goes to the table.*
What, this! and this!—what! new and old together!

Seal ? If a seraph shouted from the sun,
And bade me seal against the rights of the Church,

I would anathematize him. I will not seal.

[*Exit with* HERBERT.

Enter KING HENRY.

Henry. Where's Thomas ? hath he sign'd ?
show me the papers !
Sign'd and not seal'd ! How's that ?

John of Oxford. He would not seal.
And when he sign'd, his face was stormy red—
Shame, wrath, I know not what. He sat down
    there
And dropt it in his hands, and then a pale-
    ness,
Like the wan twilight after sunset, crept
Up even to the tonsure, and he groan'd,
" False to myself ! It is the will of God ! "
    Henry. God's will be what it will, the man
    shall seal,
Or I will seal his doom. My burgher's son—
Nay, if I cannot break him as the prelate,
I'll crush him as the subject. Send for him back.
                [*Sits on his throne.*
Barons and bishops of our realm of England,
After the nineteen winters of King Stephen—
A reign which was no reign, when none could
    sit
By his own hearth in peace ; when murder
    common
As nature's death, like Egypt's plague, had
    fill'd
All things with blood ; when every doorway
    blush'd,
Dash'd red with that unhallow'd passover ;
When every baron ground his blade in blood ;
The household dough was kneaded up with
    blood ;

The millwheel turn'd in blood ; the wholesome
    plough
Lay rusting in the furrow's yellow weeds,
Till famine dwarft the race—I came, your
    King !
Nor dwelt alone, like a soft lord of the East,
In mine own hall, and sucking thro' fools'
    ears
The flatteries of corruption—went abroad
Thro' all my counties, spied my people's
    ways ;
Yea, heard the churl against the baron—
    yea,
And did him justice ; sat in mine own courts
Judging my judges, that had found a King
Who ranged confusions, made the twilight
    day—
And struck a shape from out the vague, and
    law
From madness.   And the event—our fallows
    till'd,
Much corn, repeopled towns, a realm again.
So far my course, albeit not glassy-smooth,
Had prosper'd in the main, but suddenly
Jarr'd on this rock.   A cleric violated
The daughter of his host, and murder'd him.
Bishops—York, London, Chichester, Westmin-
    ster—
Ye haled this tonsured devil into your courts ;

But since your canon will not let you take
Life for a life, ye but degraded him
Where I had hang'd him.   What doth hard murder care
For degradation? and that made me muse,
Being bounden by my coronation oath
To do men justice.   Look to it, your own selves !
Say that a cleric murder'd an archbishop,
What could ye do?   Degrade, imprison him—
Not death for death.
   John of Oxford.   But I, my liege, could swear,
To death for death.
   Henry.   And, looking thro' my reign,
I found a hundred ghastly murders done
By men, the scum and offal of the Church ;
Then, glancing thro' the story of this realm,
I came on certain wholesome usages,
Lost in desuetude, of my grandsire's day,
Good royal customs—had them written fair
For John of Oxford here to read to you.
   John of Oxford.   And I can easily swear to these as being
The King's will and God's will and justice ; yet
I could but read a part to-day, because—
   Fitzurse.   Because my lord of Canterbury—

De Tracy.   Ay,
This lord of Canterbury—
    De Brito.   As is his wont
Too much of late whene'er your royal rights
Are mooted in our councils—
    Fitzurse.   —made an uproar.
    Henry. And Becket had my bosom on all
        this ;
If ever man by bonds of gratefulness—
I raised him from the puddle of the gutter,
I made him porcelain from the clay of the
        city—
Thought that I knew him, err'd thro' love of
        him,
Hoped, were he chosen archbishop, Church and
        Crown,
Two sisters gliding in an equal dance,
Two rivers gently flowing side by side—
But no !
The bird that moults sings the same song
        again,
The snake that sloughs comes out a snake
        again.
Snake — ay, but he that lookt a fangless
        one,
Issues a venomous adder.
For he, when having dofft the Chancellor's
        robe—
Flung the Great Seal of England in my face—

Claim'd some of our crown lands for Canter-
    bury—
My comrade, boon companion, my co-reveller,
The master of his master, the King's king.—
God's eyes! I had meant to make him all but
    king.
Chancellor-Archbishop, he might well have
    sway'd
All England under Henry, the young King,
When I was hence. What did the traitor
    say?
False to himself, but ten-fold false to me!
The will of God—why, then it is my will—
Is he coming?
    Messenger (*entering*). With a crowd of wor-
    shippers,
And holds his cross before him thro' the crowd,
As one that puts himself in sanctuary.
    Henry. His cross!
    Roger of York. His cross! I'll front him,
    cross to cross. [*Exit* ROGER OF YORK.
    Henry. His cross! it is the traitor that im-
    putes
Treachery to his King!
It is not safe for me to look upon him.
Away—with me!
        [*Goes in with his* BARONS *to the Council
           Chamber, the door of which is left
           open.*

Enter BECKET, *holding his cross of silver before
     him.   The* BISHOPS *come round him.*

> *Hereford.*   The King will not abide thee with
>   thy cross.
> Permit me, my good lord, to bear it for thee,
> Being thy chaplain.
> > *Becket.*   No : it must protect me.
> > *Herbert.*   As once he bore the standard of the
> >   Angles,
> So now he bears the standard of the angels.
> > *Foliot.*   I am the Dean of the province : let me
> >   bear it.
> Make not thy King a traitorous murderer.
> > *Becket.*   Did not your   barons draw   their
> >   swords against me ?

Enter ROGER OF YORK, *with his cross, advancing
               to* BECKET.

> *Becket.*   Wherefore dost thou presume to bear
>   thy cross,
> Against the solemn ordinance from Rome,
> Out of thy province ?
> > *Roger of York.*   Why dost thou presume,
> Arm'd with thy cross, to come before the King ?
> If Canterbury bring his cross to court,
> Let York bear his to mate with Canterbury.

Foliot (*seizing hold of* BECKET's *cross*).   Nay,
    nay, my lord, thou must not brave the King.
Nay, let me have it.   I will have it !

Becket.   Away !
                            [*Flinging him off.*

Foliot.   He fasts, they say, this mitred Her-
cules !

He fast ! is that an arm of fast ?   My lord,
Hadst thou not sign'd, I had gone along with
thee ;
But thou the shepherd hast betray'd the sheep,
And thou art perjured, and thou wilt not seal.
As Chancellor thou wast against the Church,
Now as Archbishop goest against the King ;
For, like a fool, thou knowst no middle way.
Ay, ay ! but art thou stronger than the King ?

Becket.   Strong—not in mine own self, but
Heaven ; true
To either function, holding it ; and thou
Fast, scourge thyself, and mortify thy flesh,
Not spirit—thou remainest Gilbert Foliot,
A worldly follower of the worldly strong.
I, bearing this great ensign, make it clear
Under what Prince I fight.

Foliot.   My lord of York,
Let us go in to the Council, where our bishops
And our great lords will sit in judgment on him.

Becket.   Sons sit in judgment on their father !—
then
The spire of Holy Church may prick the graves—
Her crypt among the stars.   Sign ? seal ? I
promised
The King to obey these customs, not yet written,
Saving mine order ; true too, that when written,

I sign'd them—being a fool, as Foliot call'd me.
I hold not by my signing.   Get ye hence,
Tell what I say to the King.

    [Exeunt HEREFORD, FOLIOT, *and other*
     BISHOPS.

 Roger of York.   The Church will hate thee.

            [Exit.

 Becket.   Serve my best friend and make him
  my worst foe ;
Fight for the Church, and set the Church against
  me !

 Herbert.   To be honest is to set all knaves
  against thee.
Ah ! Thomas, excommunicate them all !

 Hereford (*reëntering*).   I cannot brook the
  turmoil thou hast raised.
I would, my lord Thomas of Canterbury,
Thou wert plain Thomas and not Canterbury,
Or that thou wouldst deliver Canterbury
To our King's hands again, and be at peace.

 Hilary (*reëntering*).   For hath not thine
  ambition set the Church
This day between the hammer and the anvil—
Fealty to the King, obedience to thyself ?

 Herbert.   What say the bishops ?

 Hilary.   Some have pleaded for him,
But the King rages—most are with the King ;
And some are reeds, that one time sway to the
  current,

And to the wind another.   But we hold
Thou art forsworn ; and no forsworn Archbishop
Shall helm the Church.   We therefore place our-
    selves
Under the shield and safeguard of the Pope,
And cite thee to appear before the Pope
And   answer   thine   accusers.   .   .   Art   thou
    deaf ?
 Becket.   I hear you.   [*Clash of arms.*
 Hilary. Dost thou hear those others ?
 Becket.   Ay,
 Roger of York (reëntering).   The   King's
    "God's eyes!" come now so thick and
    fast,
We fear that he may reave thee of thine own.
Come on, come on ! it is not fit for us
To see the proud Archbishop mutilated.
Say that he blind thee and tear out thy tongue.
 Becket.   So be it.   He begins at top with me :
They crucified St. Peter downward.
 Roger of York.   Nay,
But for their sake who stagger betwixt thine
Appeal, and Henry's anger, yield.
 Becket.   Hence, Satan !
      [*Exit* ROGER OF YORK.
 Fitzurse (reëntering).   My lord, the King de-
    mands three hundred marks,
Due from his castles of Berkhamstead and Eye
When thou thereof wast warden.

Becket.   Tell the King
I spent thrice that in fortifying his castles.
De Tracy (*reëntering*).   My lord, the King de-
     mands seven hundred marks,   ˙
Lent at the siege of Toulouse by the King.
Becket.   I led seven hundred knights and
     fought his wars.
De Brito (*reëntering*).   My lord, the King de-
     mands five hundred marks,
Advanced thee at his instance by the Jews,
For which the King was bound security.
Becket.   I thought it was a gift; I thought it
     was a gift.

Enter Lord LEICESTER (*followed by* BARONS *and*
     BISHOPS).

Leicester.   My lord, I come unwillingly. The
     King
Demands a strict account of all those revenues
From all the vacant sees and abbacies
Which came into thy hands when Chancellor.
Becket.   How much might that amount to, my
     lord Leicester?
Leicester.   Some thirty—forty thousand silver
     marks.
Becket.   Are these your customs? O my good
     lord Leicester,
The King and I were brothers. All I had

I lavish'd for the glory of the King ;
I shone from him, for him, his glory, his
Reflection : now the glory of the Church
Hath swallow'd up the glory of the King ;
I am his no more, but hers.   Grant me one day
To ponder these demands.

    Leicester.   Hear first thy sentence !
The King and all his lords—

    Becket.   Son, first hear *me !*

    Leicester.   Nay, nay, canst thou, that holdest
        thine estates
In fee and barony of the King, decline
The judgment of the King ?

    Becket.   The King !   I hold
Nothing in fee and barony of the King.
Whatever the Church owns—she holds it in
Free and perpetual alms, unsubject to
One earthly sceptre.

    Leicester.   Nay, but hear thy judgment.
The King and all his barons—

    Becket.   Judgment !   Barons !
Who but the bridegroom dares to judge the bride,
Or he the bridegroom may appoint?   Not he
That is not of the house, but from the street
Stain'd with the mire thereof.

                    I had been so true
To Henry and mine office that the King
Would throne me in the great Archbishopric :
And I, that knew mine own infirmity,

For the King's pleasure rather than God's cause
Took it upon me—err'd thro' love of him.
Now therefore God from me withdraws Himself,
And the King too.
               What! forty thousand marks!
Why thou, the King, the Pope, the Saints, the
    world,
Know that when made Archbishop I was freed,
Before the Prince and chief Justiciary,
From every bond and debt and obligation
Incurr'd as Chancellor.
              Hear me, son.
                   As gold
Outvalues dross, light darkness, Abel Cain,
The soul the body, and the Church the Throne,
I charge thee, upon pain of mine anathema,
That thou obey, not me, but God in me,
Rather than Henry. I refuse to stand
By the King's censure, make my cry to the Pope,
By whom I will be judged; refer myself,
The King, these customs, all the Church, to him,
And under his authority—I depart.   [*Going.*
    [LEICESTER *looks at him doubtingly.*
Am I a prisoner?
   Leicester.   By St. Lazarus, no!
I am confounded by thee. Go in peace.
   De Broc. In peace now—but after. Take
    that for earnest.
      [*Flings a bone at him from the rushes.*

De Brito, Fitzurse, De Tracy, and others (flinging wisps of rushes).   Ay, go in peace, caitiff, caitiff!   And that too, perjured prelate—and that, turncoat shaveling!   There, there, there! traitor, traitor, traitor!

Becket.   Mannerless wolves!

　　　　　　　　　　　[Turning and facing them.

Herbert.　　　　　　　Enough, my lord, enough!

Becket.   Barons of England and of Normandy,
When what ye shake at doth but seem to fly,
True test of coward, ye follow with a yell.
But I that threw the mightiest knight of France,
Sir Engelram de Trie,—

Herbert.　　　　　　　Enough, my lord.

Becket.   More than enough.   I play the fool
　　again.

　　　　　　　Enter HERALD.

Herald.   The King commands you, upon pain
　　of death,
That none should wrong or injure your ' Arch-
　　bishop.

Foliot.   Deal gently with the young man Ab-
　　salom.

　　*[Great doors of the Hall at the back open, and
　　　discover a crowd.   They shout:*

Blessed is he that cometh in the name of the
　　Lord!

Refectory of the Monastery at Northampton. A Banquet on the Tables.

Enter BECKET. BECKET'S RETAINERS.

First Retainer. Do thou speak first?
    Second Retainer. Nay, thou! Nay, thou!
Hast not thou drawn the short straw?
    First Retainer. My lord Archbishop, wilt thou permit us—
    Becket. To speak without stammering and like a free man? Ay.
    First Retainer. My lord, permit us then to leave thy service.
    Becket. When?
    First Retainer. Now.
    Becket. To-night?
    First Retainer. To-night, my lord.
    Becket. And why?
    First Retainer. My lord, we leave thee not without tears.
    Becket. Tears? Why not stay with me then?
    First Retainer. My lord, we cannot yield thee an answer altogether to thy satisfaction.
    Becket. I warrant you, or your own either.

Shall I find you one? The King hath frowned upon me.

First Retainer. That is not altogether our answer, my lord.

Becket. No; yet all but all. Go, go! Ye have eaten of my dish and drunken of my cup for a dozen years.

First Retainer. And so we have. We mean thee no wrong. Wilt thou not say, "God bless you," ere we go?

Becket. God bless you all! God redden your pale blood! But mine is human-red; and when ye shall hear it is poured out upon earth, and see it mounting to Heaven, my God bless you, that seems sweet to you now, will blast and blind you like a curse.

First Retainer. We hope not, my lord. Our humblest thanks for your blessing. Farewell!

[*Exeunt* RETAINERS.

Becket. Farewell, friends! farewell, swallows! I wrong the bird; she leaves only the nest she built, they leave the builder. Why? Am I to be murdered to-night? [*Knocking at the door.*

Attendant. Here is a missive left at the gate by one from the Castle.

Becket. Cornwall's hand or Leicester's: they write marvellously alike. [*Reading.*

"Fly at once to France, to King Louis of France: there be those about our King who would have thy blood."

Was not my lord of Leicester bidden to our supper?

Attendant. Ay, my lord, and divers other earls and barons. But the hour is past, and our brother, Master Cook, he makes moan that all be a-getting cold.

Becket. And I make my moan along with him. Cold after warm, winter after summer, and the golden leaves, these earls and barons, that clung to me, frosted off me by the first cold frown of the King. Cold, but look how the table steams, like a heathen altar; nay, like the altar at Jerusalem. Shall God's good gifts be wasted? None of them here! Call in the poor from the streets, and let them feast.

Herbert. That is the parable of our blessed Lord.

Becket. And why should not the parable of our blessed Lord be acted again? Call in the poor! The Church is ever at variance with the kings, and ever at one with the poor. I marked a group of lazars in the market-place—half-rag, half-sore—beggars, poor rogues (Heaven bless 'em) who never saw nor dreamed of such a banquet. I will amaze them. Call them in, I say. They shall henceforward be my earls and barons —our lords and masters in Christ Jesus.

[*Exit* HERBERT.

If the King hold his purpose, I am myself a

beggar. Forty thousand marks! forty thousand devils—and these craven bishops!

A Poor Man (entering) with his dog. My lord Archbishop, may I come in with my poor friend, my dog? The King's verdurer caught him a-hunting in the forest and cut off his paws. The dog followed his calling, my lord. I ha' carried him ever so many miles in my arms, and he licks my face and moans and cries out against the King.

Becket. Better thy dog than thee. The King's courts would use thee worse than thy dog—they are too bloody. Were the Church king, it would be otherwise. Poor beast! poor beast! set him down. I will bind up his wounds with my napkin. Give him a bone, give him a bone! Who misuses a dog would misuse a child—they cannot speak for themselves. Past help! his paws are past help! God help him!

Enter the BEGGARS *(and seat themselves at the Tables).* BECKET *and* HERBERT *wait upon them.*

First Beggar. Swine, sheep, ox—here's a French supper. When thieves fall out, honest men—

Second Beggar. Is the Archbishop a thief who gives thee thy supper?

First Beggar. Well, then, how does it go?
When honest men fall out, thieves—no, it can't
be that.

Second Beggar. Who stole the widow's one
sitting hen o' Sunday,
when she was at mass?

First Beggar. Come,
come! thou hadst thy
share on her. Sitting
hen! Our Lord Becket's
our great sitting-hen cock,
and we shouldn't ha'
been sitting here if the
barons and bishops hadn't
been a-sitting on the
Archbishop.

Becket. Ay, the princes
sat in judgment against
me, and the Lord hath
prepared your table—
*Sederunt principes, ederunt
pauperes.*

A Voice. Becket, be-
ware of the knife!

Becket. Who spoke?

Third Beggar. No-
body, my lord. What's that, my lord?

Becket. Venison.

Third Beggar. Venison?

Becket. Buck ; deer, as you call it.

Third Beggar. King's meat! By the Lord, won't we pray for your lordship!

Becket. And, my children, your prayers will do more for me in the day of peril that dawns darkly and drearily over the house of God—yea, and in the day of judgment also, than the swords of the craven sycophants would have done had they remained true to me whose bread they have partaken. I must leave you to your banquet. Feed, feast, and be merry. Herbert, for the sake of the Church itself, if not for my own, I must fly to France to-night. Come with me.

　　　　　　　　　　　　[*Exit with* HERBERT.

Third Beggar. Here—all of you—my lord's health (*they drink*). Well—if that isn't goodly wine—

First Beggar. Then there isn't a goodly wench to serve him with it : they were fighting for her to-day in the street.

Third Beggar. Peace!

First Beggar.

　　The black sheep baaed to the miller's ewe lamb,
　　　　The miller's away for to-night.
　　Black sheep, quoth she, too black a sin for me.

And what said the black sheep, my masters?

　　We can make a black sin white.

Third Beggar. Peace!

First Beggar.

" Ewe lamb, ewe lamb, I am here by the dam."
   But the miller came home that night,
And so dusted his back with the meal in his sack,
   That he made the black sheep white.

Third Beggar. Be we not of the family? be
we not a-supping with the head of the family? be
we not in my lord's own refractory? Out from
among us ; thou art our black sheep.

Enter the four KNIGHTS.

Fitzurse. Sheep, said he? And sheep without the shepherd, too. Where is my lord Archbishop? Thou the lustiest and lousiest of this
Cain's brotherhood, answer.

Third Beggar. With Cain's answer, my lord.
Am I his keeper? Thou shouldst call him Cain,
not me.

Fitzurse. So I do, for he would murder his
brother the State.

Third Beggar (*rising and advancing*). No, my
lord ; but because the Lord hath set his mark
upon him that no man should murder him.

Fitzurse. Where is he ? where is he?

Third Beggar. With Cain belike, in the land
of Nod, or in the land of France for aught I
know,

Fitzurse. France ! Ha ! De Morville, Tracy,

Brito—fled is he? Cross swords all of you!
swear to follow him! Remember the Queen!

   [*The four* KNIGHTS *cross their swords.*

De Brito. They mock us; he is here.

   [*All the* BEGGARS *rise and advance*
    upon them.

Fitzurse. Come, you filthy knaves, let us pass.

Third Beggar. Nay, my lord, let *us* pass. We
be a-going home after our supper in all humble-
ness, my lord; for the Archbishop loves humble-
ness, my lord; and though we be fifty to four, we
daren't fight you with our crutches, my lord.
There now, if thou hast not laid hands upon me!
and my fellows know that I am all one scale like
a fish. I pray God I haven't given thee my leprosy,
my lord.   [FITZURSE *shrinks from him, and*
    another presses upon DE BRITO.

De Brito. Away, dog!

Fourth Beggar. And I was bit by a mad dog
o' Friday, an' I be half dog already by this token,
that tho' I can drink wine I cannot bide water, my
lord; and I want to bite, I want to bite, and they
do say the very breath catches.

De Brito. Insolent clown. Shall I smite him
with the edge of the sword?

De Morville. No, nor with the flat of it either.
Smite the shepherd and the sheep are scattered.
Smite the sheep and the shepherd will excom-
municate thee.

De Brito. Yet my fingers itch to beat him into nothing.

Fifth Beggar. So do mine, my lord. I was born with it, and sulphur won't bring it out o' me. But for all that the Archbishop washed my feet o' Tuesday. He likes it, my lord.

Sixth Beggar. And see here, my lord, this rag fro' the gangrene i' my leg. It's humbling—it smells o' human natur'. Wilt thou smell it, my lord? for the Archbishop likes the smell on it, my lord; for I be his lord and master i' Christ, my lord.

De Morville. Faugh! we shall all be poisoned. Let us go. [*They draw back,* BEGGARS *following.*

Seventh Beggar. My lord, I ha' three sisters a-dying at home o' the sweating sickness. They be dead while I be a-supping.

Eighth Beggar. And I ha' nine darters i' the spital that be dead ten times o'er i' one day wi' the putrid fever; and I bring the taint on it along wi' me, for the Archbishop likes it, my lord. [*Pressing upon the* KNIGHTS *till they disappear through the door.*

Third Beggar. Crutches, and itches, and leprosies, and ulcers, and gangrenes, and running sores, praise ye the Lord, for to-night ye have saved our Archbishop!

First Beggar. I'll go back again. I hain't half done yet.

Herbert of Bosham (*entering*). My friends, the Archbishop bids you good-night. He hath retired to rest, and being in great jeopardy of his life, he hath made his bed between the altars, from whence he sends me to bid you this night pray for him who hath fed you in the wilderness.

Third Beggar. So we will—so we will, I warrant thee. Becket shall be king, and the Holy Father shall be king, and the world shall live by the King's venison and the bread o' the Lord, and there shall be no more poor forever. Hurrah! Vive le Roy! That's the English of it.

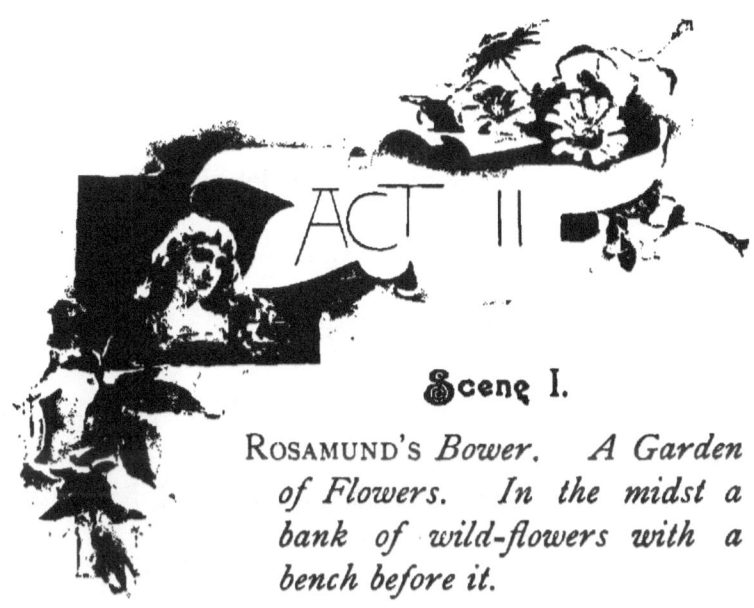

Scene I.

ROSAMUND'S *Bower.   A Garden
of Flowers.   In the midst a
bank of wild-flowers with a
bench before it.*

Voices heard singing among the trees.

Duet.

1. Is it the wind of the dawn that I hear in the pine
    overhead ?
2. No ; but the voice of the deep as it hollows the cliffs
    of the land.
1. Is there a voice coming up with the voice of the deep
    from the strand,
    One coming up with a song in the flush of the glim-
    mering red ?
2. Love that is born of the deep coming up with the
    sun from the sea.
1. Love that can shape or can shatter a life till the life
    shall have fled ?
2. Nay, let us welcome him, Love that can lift up a life
    from the dead.

1. Keep him away from the lone little isle. Let us be, let us be.
2. Nay, let him make it his own, let him reign in it—he, it is he,
    Love that is born of the deep coming up with the sun from the sea.

Enter HENRY *and* ROSAMUND.

Rosamund. Be friends with him again—I do beseech thee.

    Henry. With Becket? I have but one hour with thee—
Sceptre and crozier clashing, and the mitre
Grappling the crown—and when I flee from this
For a gasp of freer air, a breathing-while
To rest upon thy bosom and forget him—
Why thou, my bird, thou pipest Becket, Becket—
Yea, thou my golden dream of Love's own bower,
Must be the nightmare breaking on my peace
With " Becket."

    Rosamund. O my life's life, not to smile
Is all but death to me. My sun, no cloud!
Let there not be one frown in this one hour.
Out of the many thine, let this be mine !
Look rather thou all-royal as when first
I met thee.

    Henry. Where was that ?

    Rosamund. Forgetting that
Forgets me too.

Henry.   Nay, I remember it well.
There on the moors.
    Rosamund.   And in a narrow path.
A plover flew before thee.   Then I saw
Thy high black steed among the flaming furze,
Like sudden night in the main glare of day.
And from that height something was said to
     me
I knew not what.
    Henry.   I ask'd the way.
    Rosamund.   I think so.
So I lost mine.
    Henry.   Thou wast too shamed to answer.
    Rosamund.   Too scared—so young !
    Henry.   The rosebud of my rose !—
Well, well, no more of *him*—I have sent his folk,
His kin, all his belongings, overseas ;
Age, orphans, and babe-breasting mothers—all
By hundreds to him—there to beg, starve, die—
So that the fool King Louis feed them not.
The man shall feel that I can strike him yet.
    Rosamund.   Babes, orphans, mothers ! is that
     royal, Sire ?
    Henry.   And I have been as royal with the
     Church.
He shelter'd in the Abbey of Pontigny.
There wore his time studying the canon law
To work it against me.   But since he cursed
My friends at Veselay, I have let them know,

That if they keep him longer as their guest,
I scatter all their cowls to all the hells.
　　Rosamund.　And is that altogether royal?
　　Henry.　　　　Traitress!
　　Rosamund.　A faithful traitress to thy royal fame.
　　Henry.　Fame! what care I for fame?　Spite,
　　　ignorance, envy,
Yea, honesty too, paint her what way they will.
Fame of to-day is infamy to-morrow;
Infamy of to-day is fame to-morrow;
And round and round again.　What matters?
　　　Royal—
I mean to leave the royalty of my crown
Unlessen'd to mine heirs.
　　Rosamund.　　　　　　Still—thy fame too:
I say that should be royal.
　　Henry.　　　　　　And I say,
I care not for thy saying.
　　Rosamund.　　　　　And I say,
I care not for *thy* saying.　A greater King
Than thou art, Love, who cares not for the word,
Makes "care not"—care.　There have I spoken
　　　true?
　　Henry.　Care dwell with me forever, when I
　　　cease
To care for thee as ever!
　　Rosamund.　No need! no need!　.　.　.
There is a bench.　Come, wilt thou sit?　　　.
　　　My bank

Of wild-flowers [*he sits*].   At thy feet !
　　　　　　　　　　　　　　[*She sits at his feet.*

Henry.   I bade them clear
A royal pleasaunce for thee, in the wood,
Not leave these countryfolk at court.
    Rosamund.   I brought them
In from the wood, and set them here. I love
    them
More than the garden flowers, that seem at
    most
Sweet guests, or foreign cousins, not half speak-
    ing
The language of the land. I love *them* too,
Yes. But, my liege, I am sure, of all the roses—
Shame fall on those who gave it a dog's name—
This wild one (*picking a brier-rose*)—nay, I shall
    not prick myself—
Is sweetest. Do but smell !
    Henry.   Thou rose of the world !
Thou rose of all the roses !   [*Muttering.*
I am not worthy of her—this beast-body
That God has plunged my soul in—I, that taking
The Fiend's advantage of a throne, so long
Have wander'd among women,—a foul stream
Thro' fever-breeding levels,—at her side,
Among these happy dales, run clearer, drop
The mud I carried, like yon brook, and glass
The faithful face of heaven—
      [*Looking at her, and unconsciously aloud,*
            —thine ! thine !
    Rosamund.   I know it.

Henry (muttering). Not hers. We have but
    one bond, her hate of Becket.
Rosamund (half-hearing). Nay! nay! what art
    thou muttering? *I* hate Becket?
Henry (muttering). A sane and natural loath-
    ing for a soul
Purer, and truer and nobler than herself;
And mine a bitterer illegitimate hate,
A bastard hate born of a former love.
    Rosamund. My fault to name him! O let the
    hand of one
To whom thy voice is all her music, stay it
But for a breath.   *[Puts her hand before his lips.*
    Speak only of thy love.
Why there—like some loud beggar at thy gate—
The happy boldness of this hand hath won it
Love's alms, thy kiss *(looking at her hand)*—
    Sacred! I'll kiss it, too.   *[Kissing it.*
There! wherefore dost thou so peruse it? Nay,
There may be crosses in my line of life.
    Henry. Not half *her* hand—no hand to mate
    with *her,*
If it should come to that.
    Rosamund.   With her? with whom?
    Henry. Life on the hand is naked gipsy-stuff;
Life on the face, the brows—clear innocence!
Vein'd marble—not a furrow yet—and hers
                     [Muttering.
Crost and recrost, a venomous spider's web—

Rosamund (springing up). Out of the cloud,
    my Sun—out of the eclipse
Narrowing my golden hour !
Henry.   O Rosamund,
I would be true—would tell thee all—and some-
    thing
I had to say—I love thee none the less—
Which will so vex thee.
    Rosamund.   Something against *me ?*
    Henry. No, no, against myself.
    Rosamund.   I will not hear it.
Come, come, mine hour ! I bargain for mine
    hour.
I'll call thee little Geoffrey.
    Henry.   Call him !
    Rosamund.   Geoffrey !

    Enter GEOFFREY.

    Henry. How the boy grows !
    Rosamund. Ay, and his brows are thine ;
The mouth is only Clifford, my dear father.
    Geoffrey. My liege, what hast thou brought me ?
    Henry.   Venal imp !
What say'st thou to the Chancellorship of
    England ?
    Geoffrey. O yes, my liege.
    Henry. "O yes, my liege !" He speaks
As if it were a cake of gingerbread.

Dost thou know, my boy, what it is to be Chancellor of England?

Geoffrey. Something good, or thou wouldst not give it to me.

Henry. It is, my boy, to side with the King when Chancellor, and then to be made Archbishop and go against the King who made him, and turn the world upside down.

Geoffrey. I won't have it then. Nay, but give it me, and I promise thee not to turn the world upside down.

Henry (giving him a ball). Here is a ball, my boy, thy world, to turn any way and play with as thou wilt—which is more than I can do with mine. Go try it, play.   [*Exit* GEOFFREY.

A pretty lusty boy.

Rosamund.   So like to thee ;
Like to be liker.

Henry.   Not in my chin, I hope !
That threatens double.

Rosamund.   Thou art manlike perfect.

Henry. Ay, ay, no doubt ; and were I humpt
     behind,
Thou'dst say as much—the goodly way of
     women
Who love, for which I love them. May God
     grant
No ill befall or him or thee when I
Am gone.

Rosamund.   Is *he* thy enemy ?

Henry.   He ? who ? ay !

Rosamund.   Thine enemy knows the secret of
   my bower.

Henry.   And I could tear him asunder with
   wild horses

Before he would betray it.   Nay—no fear !
More like is he to excommunicate me.

Rosamund.   And I would creep, crawl over
   knife-edge flint

Barefoot, a hundred leagues, to stay his
   hand
Before he flash'd the bolt.

Henry.   And when he flash'd it
Shrink from me, like a daughter of the
   Church.

Rosamund.   Ay, but he will not.

Henry.   Ay ! but if he did ?

Rosamund.   O then ! O then ! I almost fear to
   say

That my poor heretic heart would excommuni-
   cate
His excommunication, clinging to thee
Closer than ever.

Henry (raising ROSAMUND *and kissing her).*
                              My brave-hearted Rose !

Hath he ever been to see thee ?

Rosamund.   Here ? not he.
And it is so lonely here—no confessor.

Henry. Thou shalt confess all thy sweet sins
    to me.
Rosamund. Besides, we came away in such a
    heat,
I brought not ev'n my crucifix.
Henry.   Take this.
   [*Giving her the Crucifix which* ELEANOR
    gave him.
Rosamund. O beautiful! May I have it as
    mine, till mine
Be mine again?
Henry (*thowing it round her neck*). Thine—
    as I am—till death!
Rosamund. Death? no! I'll have it with me
    in my shroud,
And wake with it, and show it to all the
    Saints.
Henry. Nay—I must go; but when thou
    layest thy lip
To this, remembering One who died for thee,
Remember also one who lives for thee
Out there in France; for I must hence to
    brave
The Pope, King Louis, and this turbulent
    priest.
Rosamund .(*kneeling*). O by thy love for me,
    all mine for thee,
Fling not thy soul into the flames of hell;
I kneel to thee—be friends with him again.

Henry.   Look, look! if little Geoffrey have
    not tost
His ball into the brook! makes after it too
To find it.   Why, the child will drown himself.

                Rosamund.   Geoffrey!
        Geoffrey !   [*Exeunt.*

Scene II.

Montmirail. " The Meeting of the Kings."
JOHN OF OXFORD *and* HENRY. *Crowd in
the distance.*

John of Oxford. You have not crown'd
    young Henry yet, my liege?
   Henry. Crown'd! by God's eyes, we
    will not have him crown'd.
I spoke of late to the boy, he answer'd me,
As if he wore the crown already—No,
We will not have him crown'd.
'Tis true what Becket told me, that the mother
Would make him play his kingship against
    mine.
   John of Oxford. Not have him crown'd?
   Henry. Not now—not yet! and Becket—
Becket should crown him were he crown'd at all :
But, since we would be lord of our own manor,
This Canterbury, like a wounded deer,
Has fled our presence and our feeding-grounds.
   John of Oxford. Cannot a smooth tongue
    lick him whole again
To serve your will?
   Henry. He hates my will, not me.
   John of Oxford. There's York, my liege.

Henry.   But England scarce would hold
Young Henry king, if only crown'd by York,
And that would stilt up York to twice himself.
There is a movement yonder in the crowd—
See if our pious—what shall I call him, John?—
Husband-in-law, our smooth-shorn suzerain,
Be yet within the field.
 John of Oxford. I will.   [*Exit.*
 Henry.   Ay! Ay!
Mince and go back! his politic Holiness
Hath all but climb'd the Roman perch again,
And we shall hear him presently with clapt wing
Crow over Barbarossa—at last tongue-free
To blast my realms with excommunication
And interdict. I must patch up a peace—
A piece in this long-tugged at, threadbare-worn
Quarrel of Crown and Church—to rend again.
His Holiness cannot steer straight thro' shoals,
Nor I. The citizen's heir hath conquer'd me
For the moment. So we make our peace with
  him.
    Enter LOUIS.

Brother of France, what shall be done with
  Becket?
 Louis. The holy Thomas! Brother, you have
  traffick'd
Between the Emperor and the Pope, between
The Pope and Antipope—a perilous game
For men to play with God.

Henry.   Ay, ay, good brother,
They call you the Monk-King.
      Louis.   Who calls me ? she
That was my wife, now yours?   You have her
      Duchy,
The point you aimed at, and pray God she
      prove
True wife to you.   You have had the better of us
In secular matters.
      Henry.   Come, confess, good brother,
You did your best or worst to keep her
      Duchy.
Only the golden Leopard printed in it
Such hold-fast claws that you perforce again
Shrank into France.   Tut, tut! did we convene
This conference but to babble of our wives ?
They are plagues enough in-door.
      Louis.   We fought in the East,
And felt the sun of Antioch scald our mail,
And push'd our lances into Saracen hearts.
We never hounded on the State at home
To spoil the Church.
      Henry.   How should you see this rightly ?
      Louis.   Well, well, no more !   I am proud of
      my " Monk-King,"
Whoever named me ; and, brother, Holy Church
May rock, but will not wreck, nor our Arch-
      bishop
Stagger on the slope decks for any rough sea

Blown by the breath of kings. We do forgive
    you
For aught you wrought against us.
                  [HENRY *holds up his hand.*
                    Nay, I pray you,
Do not defend yourself.   You will do much
To rake out all old dying heats, if you,
At my requesting, will but look into
The wrongs you did him, and restore his kin,
Reseat him on his throne of Canterbury,
Be, both, the friends you were.
    Henry.   The friends we were !
Co-mates we were, and had our sport together,
Co-kings we were, and made the laws together.
The world had never seen the like before.
You are too cold to know the fashion of it.
Well, well, we will be gentle with him, gracious—
Most gracious.

Enter BECKET, *after him,* JOHN OF OXFORD, ROGER
    OF YORK, GILBERT FOLIOT, DE BROC, FITZ-
    URSE, *etc.*

                Only that the rift he made
May close between us, here I am wholly king.
The word should come from him.
    Becket (kneeling).   Then, my dear liege,
I here deliver all this controversy
Into your royal hands.

Henry.   Ah, Thomas, Thomas,
Thou art thyself again, Thomas again.

Becket. (rising).   Saving God's honor !
Henry.   Out upon thee, man !
Saving the Devil's honor, his yes and no.
Knights, bishops, earls, this London spawn—by
      Mahound,
I had sooner have been born a Mussulman—

Less clashing with their priests—
I am half-way down the slope—will no man stay
    me?
I dash myself to pieces—I stay myself—
Puff—it is gone. You, Master Becket, you
That owe to me your power over me—
Nay, nay—
Brother of France, you have taken, cherish'd him
Who thief-like fled from his own church by night,
No man pursuing. I would have had him back.
Take heed he do not turn and rend you too:
For whatsoever may displease him—that
Is clean against God's honor—a shift, a trick
Whereby to challenge, face me out of all
My regal rights. Yet, yet—that none may
    dream
I go against God's honor—ay, or himself
In any reason, choose
A hundred of the wisest heads from England,
A hundred, too, from Normandy and Anjou:
Let these decide on what was customary
In olden days, and all the Church of France
Decide on their decision, I am content.
More, what the mightiest and the holiest
Of all his predecessors may have done
Ev'n to the least and meanest of my own,
Let him do the same to me—I am content.
    Louis. Ay, ay! the King humbles himself
      enough.

Becket (*aside*). Words! he will wriggle out
    of them like an eel
When the time serves. (*Aloud.*) My lieges
    and my lords,
The thanks of Holy Church are due to those
That went before us for their work, which we
Inheriting reap an easier harvest. Yet—
    Louis. My lord, will you be greater than the
    Saints,
More than St. Peter? whom—what is it you
    doubt?
Behold your peace at hand.
    Becket.   I say that those
Who went before us did not wholly clear
The deadly growths of earth, which Hell's own
    heat
So dwelt on that they rose and darken'd Heaven.
Yet they did much. Would God they had torn
    up all
By the hard root, which shoots again ; our trial
Had so been less ; but, seeing they were men
Defective or excessive, must we follow
All that they overdid or underdid?
Nay, if they were defective as St. Peter
Denying Christ, who yet defied the tyrant.
We hold by his defiance, not his defect.
O good son Louis, do not counsel me,
No, to suppress God's honor for the sake
Of any king that breathes. No, God forbid!

Henry.   No! God forbid! and turn me Mus-
   sulman!
No God but one, and Mahound is his prophet.
But for your Christian, look you, you shall
   have
None other God but me—me, Thomas, son
Of Gilbert Becket, London merchant.   Out!
I hear no more!   [*Exit.*
   Louis.   Our brother's anger puts him,
Poor man, beside himself—not wise.   My lord,
We have claspt your cause, believing that our
   brother
Had wrong'd you; but this day he proffer'd
   peace.
You will have war; and tho' we grant the Church
King over this world's kings, yet, my good
   lord,
We that are kings are something in this world,
And so we pray you, draw yourself from under
The wings of France.   We shelter you no more.
                                             [*Exit.*
   John of Oxford.   I am glad that France hath
      scouted him at last:
I told the Pope what manner of man he was.
                                             [*Exit.*
   Roger of York.   Yea, since he flouts the will
      of either realm,
Let either cast him away like a dead dog!
                                             [*Exit*

Foliot. Yea, let a stranger spoil his heritage,
And let another take his bishopric !   [*Exit.*
  De Broc. Our castle, my lord, belongs to
      Canterbury.
I pray you come and take it.   [*Exit.*
  Fitzurse.   When you will.   [*Exit.*
  Becket. Cursed be John of Oxford, Roger of
      York,
And Gilbert Foliot ! cursed those De Brocs
That hold our Saltwood Castle from our see !
Cursed Fitzurse, and all the rest of them
That sow this hate between my lord and
      me !
  Voices from the Crowd. Blessed be the Lord
Archbishop, who hath withstood two Kings to
their faces for the honor of God.
  Becket. Out of the mouths of babes and suck-
      lings, praise !
I thank you, sons ; when kings but hold by
      crowns,
The crowd that hungers for a crown in Heaven
Is my true king.
  Herbert.   Thy true King bade thee be
A fisher of men ; thou hast them in thy net.
  Becket. I am too like the King here ; both
      of us
Too headlong for our office. Better have been
A fisherman at Bosham, my good Herbert,
Thy birthplace—the sea-creek—the petty rill

That falls into it—the green field—the gray
    church—
The simple lobster-basket, and the mesh—
The more or less of daily labor done—
The pretty gaping bills in the home-nest
Piping for bread—the daily want supplied—
The daily pleasure to supply it.
    Herbert.   Ah, Thomas,
You had not borne it, no, not for a day.
    Becket. Well, maybe, no.
    Herbert.   But bear with Walter Map,
For here he comes to comment on the time.

Enter WALTER MAP.

Walter Map. Pity, my lord, that you have
quenched the warmth of France toward you, tho'
His Holiness, after much smouldering and smok-
ing, be kindled again upon your quarter.

    Becket. Ay, if he do not end in smoke again.

    Walter Map. My lord, the fire, when first
kindled, said to the smoke, "Go up, my son,
straight to Heaven." And the smoke said, "I
go;" but anon the Northeast took and turned
him Southwest, then the Southwest turned him
Northeast, and so of the other winds; but it was
in him to go up straight if the time had been
quieter. Your lordship affects the unwavering
perpendicular; but His Holiness, pushed one way

by the Empire and another by England, if he
move at all, Heaven stay him, is fain to diagonalize.

Herbert. Diagonalize ! thou art a word-monger !
Our Thomas never will diagonalize.
Thou art a jester and a verse-maker.
Diagonalize !

Walter Map. Is the world any the worse for my
verses if the Latin rhymes be rolled out from a
full mouth ? or any harm done to the people if my
jest be in defence of the Truth ?

Becket. Ay, if the jest be so done that the
people
Delight to wallow in the grossness of it,
Till Truth herself be shamed of her defender.
Non defensoribus istis, Walter Map.

Walter Map. Is that my case ? so if the city
be sick, and I cannot call the kennel sweet, your
lordship would suspend me from verse-writing, as
you suspended yourself after sub-writing to the
customs.

Becket. I pray God pardon mine infirmity !

Walter Map. Nay, my lord, take heart ; for
tho' you suspended yourself, the Pope let you
down again ; and tho' you suspended Foliot or
another, the Pope will not leave them in suspense,
for the Pope himself is always in suspense, like
Mahound's coffin hung between heaven and earth
—always in suspense, like the scales, till the

weight of Germany or the gold of England brings
one of them down to the dust—always in suspense,
like the tail of the horologe—to and fro—tick-tack
—we make the time, we keep the time, ay, and
we serve the time ; for I have heard say that if
you boxed the Pope's ears with a purse, you
might stagger him, but he would pocket the purse.
No saying of mine—Jocelyn of Salisbury. But
the King hath bought half the College of Red-hats.
He warmed to you to-day, and you have chilled
him again. Yet you both love God. Agree with
him quickly again, even for the sake of the Church.
My one grain of good counsel which you will not
swallow. I hate a split between old friendships
as I hate the dirty gap in the face of a Cistercian
monk, that will swallow anything. Farewell.

                                    [*Exit.*
   Becket.   Map scoffs at Rome. I all but hold
     with Map.
Save for myself no Rome were left in England,
All had been his. Why should this Rome, this
     Rome,
Still choose Barabbas rather than the Christ,
Absolve the left-hand thief and damn the right?
Take fees of tyranny, wink at sacrilege,
Which even Peter had not dared? condemn
The blameless exile ?—
   Herbert.   Thee, thou holy Thomas !
I would that thou hadst been the Holy Father.

Becket. I would have done my most to keep
   Rome holy,
I would have made Rome know she still is
   Rome—
Who stands aghast at her eternal self
And shakes at mortal kings—her vacillation,
Avarice, craft—O God, how many an innocent
Has left his bones upon the way to Rome
Unwept, uncared for. Yea—on mine own self
The King had had no power except for Rome.
'Tis not the King who is guilty of mine exile,
But Rome, Rome, Rome !
   Herbert.   My lord, I see this Louis
Returning, ah ! to drive thee from his realm.
   Becket. He said as much before. Thou art
   no prophet,
Nor yet a prophet's son.
   Herbert.   Whatever he say,
Deny not thou God's honor for a king.
The King looks troubled.

Reënter KING LOUIS.

   Louis.   My dear lord Archbishop,
I learn but now that those poor Poitevins,
That in thy cause were stirr'd against King Henry,
Have been, despite his kingly promise given
To our own self of pardon, evilly used
And put to pain. I have lost all trust in him.

The Church alone hath eyes—and now I see
That I was blind—suffer the phrase—surrender-
ing
God's honor to the pleasure of a man.
Forgive me and absolve me, holy father. [*Kneels.*

     Becket. Son, I
     absolve thee in
     the name of
     God.
    Louis (*rising*). Re-
    turn to Sens,
    where we will
    care for you.
   The wine and wealth
   of all our France
   are yours;
   Rest in our realm,
   and be at peace
   with all.
     [*Exeunt.*
    *Voices from
    the Crowd.*
   Long live the
   good King

Louis ! God bless the great Archbishop!

Reënter HENRY *and* JOHN OF OXFORD.

Henry (*looking after* KING LOUIS *and* BECKET).
Ay, there they go—both backs are turned to me—

Why then I strike into my former path
For England, crown young Henry there, and make
Our waning Eleanor all but love me!
                                        John,
Thou hast served me heretofore with Rome—and well.
They call thee John the Swearer.
   John of Oxford.   For this reason,
That, being ever duteous to the King,
I evermore have sworn upon his side,
And ever mean to do it.
   Henry (claps him on the shoulder).   Honest John!
To Rome again! the storm begins again.
Spare not thy tongue! be lavish with our coins,
Threaten our junction with the Emperor—flatter
And fright the Pope—bribe all the Cardinals—leave
Lateran and Vatican in one dust of gold—
Swear and unswear, state and misstate thy best!
I go to have young Henry crown'd by York.

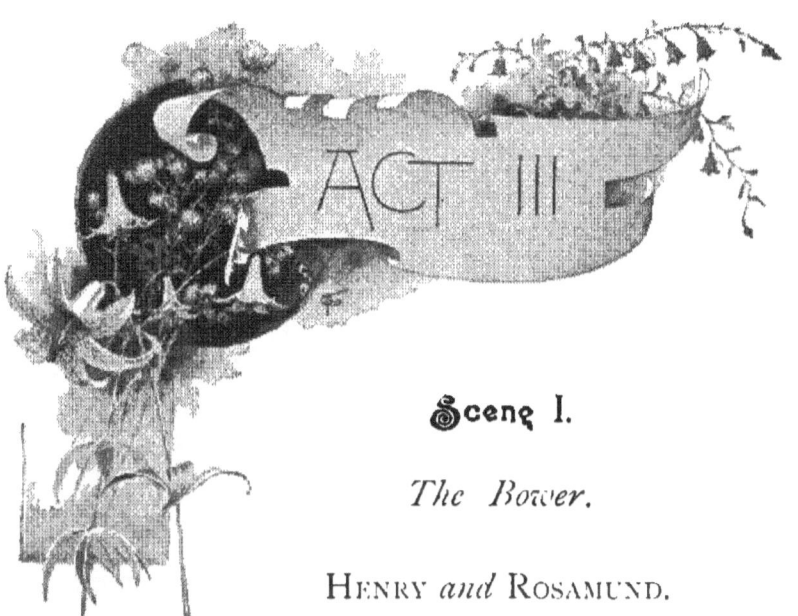

Scene I.

The Bower.

HENRY *and* ROSAMUND.

Henry. All that you say is just. I cannot answer it
Till better times, when I shall put away—
Rosamund. What will you put away?
Henry. That which you ask me
Till better times. Let it content you now
There is no woman that I love so well.
Rosamund. No woman but should be content
with that—
Henry. And one fair child to fondle!
Rosamund. O yes, the child
We waited for so long—Heaven's gift at last—
And how you doated on him then! To-day
I almost fear'd your kiss was colder—yes—
But then the child *is* such a child. What chance

That he should ever spread into the man
Here in our silence?   I have done my best.
I am not learn'd.

Henry.   I am the King, his father.
And I will look to it.   Is our secret ours?
Have you had any alarm?   no stranger?

Rosamund.   No.
The warder of the bower hath given himself
Of late to wine.   I sometimes think he sleeps
When he should watch ; and yet what fear? the
        people
Believe the wood enchanted.   No one comes,
Nor foe nor friend ; his fond excess of wine
Springs from the loneliness of my poor bower,
Which weighs even on me.

Henry.   Yet these tree-towers,
Their long bird-echoing minster-aisles,—the voice
Of the perpetual brook, these golden slopes
Of Solomon-shaming flowers—that was your
        saying,
All pleased you so at first.

Rosamund.   Not now so much.
My Anjou bower was scarce as beautiful.
But you were oftener there.   I have none but
        you.
The brook's voice is not yours, and no flower, not
The sun himself, should he be changed to one,
Could shine away the darkness of that gap
Left by the lack of love !

Henry. The lack of love !

Rosamund. Of one we love. Nay, I would not be bold,
Yet hoped ere this you might—
                [Looks earnestly at him.

Henry. Anything further ?

Rosamund. Only my best bower-maiden died of late,
And that old priest whom John of Salisbury trusted
Hath sent another.

Henry. Secret ?

Rosamund. I but ask'd her
One question, and she primm'd her mouth and put
Her hands together—thus—and said, God help her,
That she was sworn to silence.

Henry. What did you ask her ?

Rosamund. Some daily something-nothing.

Henry. Secret, then ?

Rosamund. I do not love her. Must you go, my liege,
So suddenly ?

Henry. I came to England suddenly,
And on a great occasion sure to wake
As great a wrath in Becket—

Rosamund. Always Becket !
He always comes between us.

Henry.   —And to meet it
I needs must leave as suddenly.   It is raining,
Put on your hood and see me to the bounds.

                                    [*Exeunt.*

Margery (*singing behind scene*).

> Babble in bower
>   Under the rose!
> Bee mustn't buzz,
>   Whoop—but he knows.
>
> Kiss me, little one,
>   Nobody near !
> Grasshopper, grasshopper,
>   Whoop—you can hear.
>
> Kiss in the bower,
>   Tit on the tree!
> Bird mustn't tell,
>   Whoop—he can see.

Enter MARGERY.

I ha' been but a week here and I ha' seen
what I ha' seen, for to be sure it's no more than
a week since our old Father Philip that has con-
fessed our mother for twenty years, and she was
hard put to it, and to speak truth, nigh at the end
of our last crust, and that mouldy, and she cried
out on him to put me forth in the world and to
make me a woman of the world, and to win my
own bread, whereupon he asked our mother if I

could keep a quiet tongue i' my head, and not speak till I was spoke to, and I answered for myself that I never spoke more than was needed, and he told me he would advance me to the service of a great lady, and took me ever so far away, and gave me a great pat o' the cheek for a pretty wench, and said it was a pity to blindfold such eyes as mine, and such to be sure they be, but he blinded 'em for all that, and so brought me no-hows as I may say, and the more shame to him after his promise, into a garden and not into the world, and bade me whatever I saw not to speak one word, an' it 'ud be well for me in the end, for there were great ones who would look after me, and to be sure I ha' seen great ones to-day—and then not to speak one word, for that's the rule o' the garden, tho' to be sure if I had been Eve i' the garden I shouldn't ha' minded the apple, for what's an apple, you know, save to a child, and I'm no child, but more a woman o' the world than my lady here, and I ha' seen what I ha' seen—tho' to be sure if I hadn't minded it we should all on us ha' had to go, bless the Saints, wi' bare backs, but the backs 'ud ha' countenanced one another, and belike it 'ud ha' been always summer, and anyhow I am as well-shaped as my lady here, and I ha' seen what I ha' seen, and what's the good of my talking to myself, for here comes my lady (*Enter* ROSAMUND),

and, my lady, tho' I shouldn't speak one word, I
wish you joy o' the King's brother.

Rosamund. What is it you mean?

Margery. I mean your goodman, your husband, my lady, for I saw your ladyship a-parting wi' him even now i' the coppice, when I was a-getting o' bluebells for your ladyship's nose to smell on—and I ha' seen the King once at Oxford, and he's as like the King as finger-nail to finger-nail, and I thought at first it was the King, only you know the King's married, for King Louis—

Rosamund. Married!

Margery. Years and years, my lady, for her husband, King Louis—

Rosamund. Hush!

Margery.—And I thought if it were the King's brother he had a better bride than the King, for the people do say that his is bad beyond all reckoning, and—

Rosamund. The people lie.

Margery. Very like, my lady, but most on 'em know an honest woman and a lady when they see her, and besides they say, she makes songs, and that's against her, for I never knew an honest woman that could make songs, tho' to be sure our mother 'ill sing me old songs by the hour, but then, God help her, she had 'em from her mother, and her mother from her mother back and back for ever so long, but none on 'em ever made songs, and they were all honest.

Rosamund. Go, you shall tell me of her some other time.

Margery. There's none so much to tell on her, my lady, only she kept the seventh commandment better than some I know on, or I couldn't look your ladyship i' the face, and she brew'd the best ale in all Glo'ster, that is to say in her time when she had the " Crown."

Rosamund. The crown! who?

Margery. Mother.

Rosamund. I mean her whom you call— fancy—my husband's brother's wife.

Margery. Oh, Queen Eleanor. Yes, my lady ; and tho' I be sworn not to speak a word, I can tell you all about her, if—

Rosamund. No word now. I am faint and sleepy. Leave me. Nay—go.
What ! will you anger me ?   [*Exit* MARGERY.
He charged me not to question any of those
About me.   Have I ? no ! she question'd *me*.
Did she not slander *him ?* Should she stay here ?
May she not tempt me, being at my side,
To question *her ?*   Nay, can I send her hence
Without his kingly leave ?   I am in the dark.
I have lived, poor bird, from cage to cage, and known
Nothing but him—happy to know no more,
So that he loved me—and he loves me—yes,
And bound me by his love to secrecy

Till his own time.

Eleanor, Eleanor, have I

Not heard ill things of her in France? Oh,
she's

The Queen of France. I see it—some con-
fusion,

Some strange mistake. I did not hear aright,

Myself confused with parting from the King.

Margery (*behind scene*).

Bee mustn't buzz,
Whoop—but he knows.

Rosamund. Yet her—what her? he hinted of
some her—

When he was here before—

Something that would displease me. Hath he
stray'd

From love's clear path into the common bush,

And, being scratch'd, returns to his true rose,

Who hath not thorn enough to prick him for
it,

Ev'n with a word?

Margery (*behind scene*).

Bird mustn't tell,
Whoop—he can see.

Rosamund. I would not hear him. Nay—
there's more—he frowned

" No mate for her, if it should come to that "—
To that—to what ?
Margery (*behind scene*).

> Whoop—but he knows,
> Whoop—but he knows.

Rosamund.   O God ! some dreadful truth is
    breaking on me—
Some dreadful thing is coming on me.

Enter GEOFFREY.

                                        Geoffrey !
Geoffrey.   What are you crying for, when the
    sun shines ?
Rosamund.   Hath not thy father left us to our-
    selves ?
Geoffrey.   Ay, but he's taken the rain with
him.   I hear Margery : I'll go play with her.
                            [*Exit* GEOFFREY.
Rosamund.

> Rainbow, stay,
> Gleam upon gloom,
> Bright as my dream,
> Rainbow, stay !
> But it passes away,
> Gloom upon gleam,
> Dark as my doom—
> O rainbow, stay.

Scene II.

Outside the Woods near ROSAMUND'S *Bower.*

ELEANOR. FITZURSE.

Eleanor.   Up from the salt lips of the land we
          two
       Have track'd the King to this dark inland
          wood ;
And somewhere hereabouts he vanish'd.   Here
His turtle builds : his exit is our adit :
Watch ! he will out again, and presently,
Seeing he must to Westminster and crown
Young Henry there to-morrow.
    Fitzurse.   We have watch'd
So long in vain, he hath pass'd out again,
And on the other side.   [*A great horn winded.*
                    Hark ! Madam !
    Eleanor.   Ay,
How ghostly sounds that horn in the black wood !
                    [*A Countryman flying.*
Whither away, man ? what are you flying from ?
    Countryman.   The witch ! the witch ! she sits
naked by a great heap of gold in the middle of
the wood, and when the horn sounds she comes
out as a wolf.   Get you hence ! a man passed in

there to-day : I holla'd to him, but he didn't hear me : he'll never out again, the witch has got him. I daren't stay—I daren't stay !

Eleanor. Kind of the witch to give thee warning tho'.   [*Man flies.*
Is not this wood-witch of the rustic's fear
Our woodland Circe that hath witch'd the King ?
    [*Horn sounded. Another flying.*

Fitzurse. Again ! stay, fool, and tell me why thou fliest.

Countryman. Fly thou too. The King keeps his forest head of game here, and when that horn sounds, a score of wolf-dogs are let loose that will tear thee piecemeal. Linger not till the third horn. Fly !   [*Exit.*

Eleanor. This is the likelier tale. We have hit the place.
Now let the King's fine game look to itself.
     [*Horn.*

Fitzurse. Again !—
And far on in the dark heart of the wood
I hear the yelping of the hounds of hell.

Eleanor. I have my dagger here to still their throats.

Fitzurse. Nay, Madam, not to-night — the night is falling.
What can be done to-night ?

Eleanor.   Well—well—away.

Traitor's Meadow at Fréteval. Pavilions and tents of the English and French Baronage.

BECKET *and* HERBERT OF BOSHAM.

Becket. See here!
    Herbert. What's here?
    Becket. A notice from the priest,
To whom our John of Salisbury committed
The secret of the bower, that our wolf-Queen
Is prowling round the fold. I should be back
In England ev'n for this.
    Herbert. These are by-things
In the great cause.
    Becket. The by-things of the Lord
Are the wrong'd innocences that will cry
From all the hidden by-ways of the world
In the great day against the wronger. I know
Thy meaning. Perish she, I, all, before
The Church should suffer wrong!
    Herbert. Do you see, my lord,
There is the King talking with Walter Map?
    Becket. He hath the Pope's last letters, and
        they threaten
The immediate thunder-blast of interdict:

Yet he can scarce be touching upon those,
Or scarce would smile that fashion.
 Herbert.   Winter sunshine!
Beware of opening out thy bosom to it,
Lest thou, myself, and all thy flock should catch
An after ague-fit of trembling. Look!
He bows, he bares his head, he is coming hither,
Still with a smile.

   Enter KING HENRY *and* WALTER MAP.

 Henry. We have had so many hours together,
  Thomas,
So many happy hours alone together,
That I would speak with you once more alone.
 Becket. My liege, your will and happiness are
  mine.   [*Exeunt* KING *and* BECKET.
 Herbert. The same smile still.
 Walter Map. Do you see that great black
cloud that hath come over the sun and cast us all
into shadow?
 Herbert. And feel it too.
 Walter Map. And see you yon side-beam that
is forced from under it, and sets the church-tower
over there all a-hell-fire, as it were?
 Herbert. Ay.
 Walter Map. It is this black, bell-silencing,
anti-marrying, burial-hindering interdict that hath
squeezed out this side-smile upon Canterbury,

whereof may come conflagration.   Were I
Thomas, I wouldn't trust it.   Sudden change is a
house on sand; and tho' I count Henry honest
enough, yet when fear creeps in at the front,
honesty steals out at the back, and the King at
last is fairly scared by this cloud—this interdict.
I have been more for the King than the Church
in this matter—yea, even for the sake of the
Church : for, truly, as the case stood, you
had safelier have slain an archbishop than a
she-goat: but our recoverer and upholder of
customs hath in this crowning of young Henry by
York and London so violated the immemorial
usage of the Church, that, like the grave-digger's
child I have heard of, trying to ring the bell, he
hath half-hanged himself in the rope of the
Church, or rather pulled all the Church with the
Holy Father astride on it down upon his own
head.

Herbert.   Were you there?

Walter Map.   In the church rope?—no.   I
was at the crowning, for I have pleasure in the
pleasure of crowds, and to read the faces of men
at a great show.

Herbert.   And how did Roger of York com-
port himself?

Walter Map.   As magnificently and archi-
episcopally as our Thomas would have done ;
only there was a dare-devil in his eye—I should

say a dare-Becket. He thought less of two
kings than of one Roger, the king of the occasion.
Foliot is the holier man, perhaps the better.
Once or twice there ran a twitch across his face,
as who should say what's to follow? but Salisbury
was a calf cowed by Mother Church, and every
now and then glancing about him like a thief at
night when he hears a door open in the house and
thinks "the master."

Herbert. And the father-king?

Walter Map. The father's eye was so tender
it would have called a goose off the green, and
once he strove to hide his face, like the Greek
king when his daughter was sacrificed, but he
thought better of it : it was but the sacrifice of a
kingdom to his son, a smaller matter; but as to
the young crownling himself, he looked so mala-
pert in the eyes, that had I fathered him I had
given him more of the rod than the sceptre.
Then followed the thunder of the captains and
the shouting, and so we came on to the banquet,
from whence there puffed out such an incense of
unctuosity into the nostrils of our Gods of Church
and State, that Lucullus or Apicius might have
sniffed it in their Hades of heathenism, so that
the smell of their own roast had not come across
it—

Herbert. Map, tho' you make your butt too
big, you overshoot it.

Walter Map. —For as to the fish, they de-
miracled the miraculous draught, and might have
sunk a navy—

Herbert. There again, Goliazing and Goliath-
izing !

Walter Map. —And as for the flesh at table,
a whole Peter's sheet, with all manner of game,
and four-footed things, and fowls—

Herbert. And all manner of creeping things
too ?

Walter Map. —Well, there were Abbots—
but they did not bring their women ; and so we
were dull enough at first, but in the end we flour-
ished out into a merriment ; for the old King
would act servitor and hand a dish to his son ;
whereupon my Lord of York—his fine-cut face
bowing and beaming with all that courtesy which
hath less loyalty in it than the backward scrape of
the clown's heel—"great honor," says he, "from
the King's self to the King's son." Did you hear
the young King's quip ?

Herbert. No, what was it ?

Walter Map. Glancing at the days when his
father was only Earl of Anjou, he answered :
"Should not an earl's son wait on a king's son ?"
And when the cold corners of the King's mouth
began to thaw, there was a great motion of
laughter among us, part real, part childlike, to be
freed from the dulness—part royal, for King and

kingling both laughed, and so we could not but
laugh, as by a royal necessity—part childlike
again—when we felt we had laughed too long
and could not stay ourselves—many midriff-
shaken even to tears, as springs gush out after
earthquakes—but from those, as I said before,
there may come a conflagration—tho', to keep the
figure moist and make it hold water, I should say
rather, the lachrymation of a lamentation ; but
look if Thomas have not flung himself at the
King's feet. They have made it up again—for
the moment.

Herbert. Thanks to the blessed Magdalen,
whose day it is.

Reënter HENRY *and* BECKET. (*During their conference the* BARONS *and* BISHOPS *of* FRANCE
and ENGLAND *come in at back of stage.*)

Becket. Ay, King ! for in thy kingdom, as thou
    knowest,
The spouse of the Great King, thy King, hath
    fallen—
The daughter of Zion lies beside the way—
The priests of Baal tread her underfoot—
The golden ornaments are stolen from her—
    Henry. Have I not promised to restore her,
    Thomas,
And send thee back again to Canterbury ?

Becket.   Send back again those exiles of my kin
Who wander famine-wasted thro' the world.
    Henry.   Have I not promised, man, to send
      them back?
    Becket.   Yet one thing more.   Thou hast
      broken thro' the pales
Of privilege, crowning thy young son by York,
London, and Salisbury—not Canterbury.
    Henry.   York crown'd the Conqueror—not
      Canterbury.
    Becket.   There was no Canterbury in William's
      time.
    Henry.   But Hereford, you know, crown'd the
      first Henry.
    Becket.   But Anselm crown'd this Henry o'er
      again.
    Henry.   And thou shalt crown my Henry o'er
      again.
    Becket.   And is it then with thy good-will that I
Proceed against thine evil councillors,
And hurl the dread ban of the Church on those
Who made the second mitre play the first,
And acted me?
    Henry.   Well, well, then—have thy way!
It may be they were evil councillors.
What more, my lord Archbishop?   What more,
      Thomas?
I make thee full amends.   Say all thy say,
But blaze not out before the Frenchmen here.

Becket. More? Nothing, so thy promise be
    thy deed.
Henry (*holding out his hand*). Give me thy
    hand. My Lords of France and England,
My friend of Canterbury and myself
Are now once more at perfect amity.
Unkingly should I be, and most unknightly,
Not striving still, however much in vain,
To rival him in Christian charity.
Herbert. All praise to Heaven, and sweet St.
    Magdalen !
Henry. And so farewell until we meet in
    England.
Becket. I fear, my liege, we may not meet in
    England.
Henry. How, do you make me a traitor?
Becket.   No, indeed !
That be far from thee.
Henry.   Come, stay with us, then,
Before you part for England.
Becket.   I am bound
For that one hour to stay with good King Louis,
Who helpt me when none else.
Herbert.   He said thy life
Was not one hour's worth in England save
King Henry gave thee first the kiss of peace.
Henry. He said so? Louis, did he? look
    you, Herbert.
When I was in mine anger with King Louis,

I sware I would not give the kiss of peace,
Not on French ground, nor any ground but
    English,
Where his cathedral stands. Mine old friend,
    Thomas,
I would there were that perfect trust between
    us,
That health of heart, once ours, ere Pope or
    King
Had come between us! Even now — who
    knows?—
I might deliver all things to thy hand—
If . . . but I say no more . . . farewell, my lord.
    Becket.   Farewell, my liege!
              [*Exit* HENRY, *then the* BARONS
              and BISHOPS.
    Walter Map.   There again! when the full
fruit of the royal promise might have dropt into
thy mouth hadst thou but opened it to thank him.
    Becket.   He fenced his royal promise with an
    if.
    Walter Map.   And is the King's *if* too high a
stile for your lordship to overstep and come at all
things in the next field?
    Becket.   Ay, if this *if* be like the Devil's "*if*
Thou wilt fall down and worship me."
    Herbert.   Oh, Thomas,
I could fall down and worship thee, my Thomas,
For thou hast trodden this wine-press alone.

Becket. Nay, of the people there are many with me.

Walter Map. I am not altogether with you, my lord, tho' I am none of those that would raise a storm between you, lest ye should draw together like two ships in a calm. You wrong the King : he meant what he said to-day. Who shall vouch for his to-morrows? One word further. Doth not the *fewness* of anything make the fulness of it in estimation? Is not virtue prized mainly for its rarity, and great baseness loathed as an exception : for were all, my lord, as noble as yourself, who would look up to you? and were all as base as—who shall I say—Fitzurse and his following—who would look down upon them? My lord, you have put so many of the King's household out of communion, that they begin to smile at it.

Becket. At their peril, at their peril—

Walter Map. —For tho' the drop may hollow out the dead stone, doth not the living skin thicken against perpetual whippings? This is the second grain of good counsel I ever proffered thee, and so cannot suffer by the rule of frequency. Have I sown it in salt? I trust not, for before God I promise you the King hath many more wolves than he can tame in his woods of England, and if it suit their purpose to howl for the King, and you still move against him, you

may have no less than to die for it ; but God and
his free wind grant your lordship a happy home-
return and the King's kiss of peace in Kent.
Farewell ! I must follow the King.   [*Exit.*
 Herbert. Ay, and I warrant the customs. Did
  the King
Speak of the customs ?
 Becket.   No !—to die for it—
I live to die for it, I die to live for it.
The State will die, the Church can never die.
The King's not like to die for that which dies ;
But I must die for that which never dies.
It will be so—my visions in the Lord :
It must be so, my friend ! the wolves of England
Must murder her one shepherd, that the sheep
May feed in peace. False figure, Map would
  say.
Earth's falses are heaven's truths. And when my
  voice
Is martyr'd mute, and this man disappears,
That perfect trust may come again between us,
And there, there, there, not here, I shall rejoice
To find my stray sheep back within the fold.
The crowd are scattering, let us move away !
And thence to England.   [*Exeunt.*

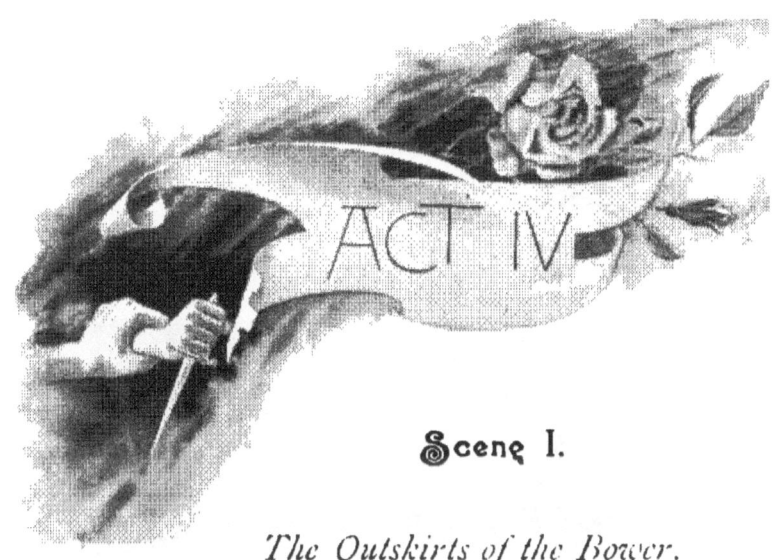

ACT IV

Scene I.

The Outskirts of the Bower.

Geoffrey (*coming out of the wood*). Light
again! light again! Margery? no,
that's a finer thing there. How it
glitters!

Eleanor (*entering*). Come to me, little one.
How camest thou hither?

Geoffrey. On my legs.

Eleanor. And mighty pretty legs, too.
Thou art the prettiest child I ever saw.
Wilt thou love me?

Geoffrey. No; I only love mother.

Eleanor. Ay; and who is thy mother?

Geoffrey. They call her—But she lives secret,
you see.

Eleanor. Why?

Geoffrey.   Don't know why.

Eleanor.   Ay, but some one comes to see her
now and then.   Who is he?

Geoffrey.   Can't tell.

Eleanor.   What does she call him?

Geoffrey.   My liege.

Eleanor.   Pretty one, how camest thou?

Geoffrey.   There was a bit of yellow silk here
and there, and it looked pretty like a glowworm,
and I thought if I followed it I should find the
fairies.

Eleanor. I am the fairy, pretty one, a good fairy to thy mother. Take me to her.

Geoffrey. There are good fairies and bad fairies, and sometimes she cries, and can't sleep sound o' nights, because of the bad fairies.

Eleanor. She shall cry no more ; she shall sleep sound enough if thou wilt take me to her. I am her good fairy.

Geoffrey. But you don't look like a good fairy. Mother does. You are not pretty, like mother.

Eleanor. We can't all of us be as pretty as thou art—(*aside*) little bastard. Come, here is a golden chain I will give thee if thou wilt lead me to thy mother.

Geoffrey. No—no gold. Mother says gold spoils all. Love is the only gold.

Eleanor. I love thy mother, my pretty boy. Show me where thou camest out of the wood.

Geoffrey. By this tree ; but I don't know if I can find the way back again.

Eleanor. Where's the warder?

Geoffrey. Very bad. Somebody struck him.

Eleanor. Ay? who was that ?

Geoffrey. Can't tell. But I heard say he had had a stroke, or you'd have heard his horn before now. Come along, then ; we shall see the silk here and there, and I want my supper. [*Exeunt.*

Scene II.

ROSAMUND'S *Bower*.

Rosamund. The boy so late ; pray God, he
  be not lost.
     I sent this Margery, and she comes
       not back ;
I sent another, and she comes not back ;
I go myself—so many alleys, crossings,
Paths, avenues—nay, if I lost him, now
The folds have fallen from the mystery,
And left all naked, I were lost indeed.

Enter GEOFFREY *and* ELEANOR.

Geoffrey, the pain thou hast put me to !
                    [*Seeing* ELEANOR.
                         Ha, you !
How came you hither ?
  Eleanor. Your own child brought me hither !
  Geoffrey. You said you couldn't trust Margery,
and I watched her and followed her into the woods,
and I lost her and went on and on till I found the
light and the lady, and she says she can make you
sleep o' nights.

Rosamund. How dared you ? Know you not
    this bower is secret,
Of and belonging to the King of England,
More sacred than his forests for the chase ?
Nay, nay, Heaven help you ; get you hence in
    haste
Lest worse befall you.
    Eleanor.   Child, I am mine own self
Of and belonging to the King. The King
Hath divers ofs and ons, ofs and belong-
    ings,
Almost as many as your true Mussulman—
Belongings, paramours, whom it pleases him
To call his wives ; but so it chances, child,
That I am his main paramour, his sultana.
But since the fondest pair of doves will jar,
Ev'n in a cage of gold, we had words o'
    late,
And thereupon he call'd my children bastards.
Do you believe that you are married to
    him ?
    Rosamund. I *should* believe it.
    Eleanor.   You must not believe it,
Because I have a wholesome medicine here
Puts that belief asleep. Your answer, beauty !
Do you believe that you are married to
    him ?
    Rosamund. Geoffrey, my boy, I saw the ball
you lost in the fork of the great willow over

the brook. Go. See that you do not fall
in. Go.

Geoffrey. And leave you alone with the good
fairy. She calls you beauty, but I don't like her
looks. Well, you bid me go, and I'll have my
ball anyhow. Shall I find you asleep when I
come back?

Rosamund. Go.   [*Exit* GEOFFREY.

Eleanor. He is easily found again. *Do* you
    believe it?
I pray you then to take my sleeping-draught;
But if you should not care to take it—see!

[*Draws a dagger.*

What! have I scared the red rose from your
    face
Into your heart? But this will find it
    there,
And dig it from the root forever.

Rosamund.   Help! help!

Eleanor. They say that walls have ears; but
    these, it seems,
Have none—and I have none to pity thee.

Rosamund. I do beseech you—my child is so
    young,
So backward too; I cannot leave him
    yet.
I am not so happy I could not die myself,
But the child is so young. You have children—
    his;

And mine is the King's child; so, if you love
    him—
Nay, if you love him, there is great wrong
    done
Somehow ; but if you do not — there are
    those
Who say you do not love him — let me
    go
With my young boy, and I will hide my
    face,
Blacken and gipsyfy it ; none shall know
    me ;
The King shall never hear of me again,
But I will beg my bread along the world
With my young boy, and God will be our
    guide.
I never meant you harm in any way.
See, I can say no more.

    Eleanor. Will you not say you are not mar-
    ried to him ?
    Rosamund. Ay, Madam, I can *say* it, if you
    will.
    Eleanor. Then is thy pretty boy a bastard?
    Rosamund.   No.
    Eleanor. And thou thyself a proven wanton?
    Rosamund.   No.
I am none such. I never loved but one.
I have heard of such that range from love to
    love,

Like the wild beast—if you can call it love.
I have heard of such — yea, even among
        those
Who sit on thrones—I never saw any such,
Never knew any such, and howsoever
You do misname me, match'd with any
        such,
I am snow to mud.
    Eleanor.   The more the pity then
That thy true home—the heavens—cry out for
        thee
Who art too pure for earth.

                Enter FITZURSE.

    Fitzurse.   Give her to me.
    Eleanor.   The Judas-lover of our passion-play
Hath track'd us hither.
    Fitzurse.   Well, why not ?   I follow'd
You and the child : he babbled all the
        way.
Give her to me to make my honeymoon.
    Eleanor.   Ay, as the bears love honey.
        Could you keep her
Indungeon'd from one whisper of the wind,
Dark even from a side glance of the moon,
And oublietted in the centre—No !
I follow out my hate and thy revenge.

Fitzurse. You bade me take revenge another
    way—
To bring her to the dust. . . . Come with me,
    love,
And I will love thee. . . . Madam, let her
    live.
I have a far-off burrow where the King
Would miss her and forever.
    Eleanor.   How sayst thou, sweetheart?
Wilt thou go with him? he will marry thee.
    Rosamund. Give me the poison; set me free
    of him!   [ELEANOR *offers the vial.*
No, no! I will not have it.
    Eleanor.   Then this other,
The wiser choice, because my sleeping-draught
May bloat thy beauty out of shape, and
    make
Thy body loathsome even to thy child;
While this but leaves thee with a broken
    heart,
A doll-face blanch'd and bloodless, over which
If pretty Geoffrey do not break his own,
It must be broken for him.
    Rosamund.   O I see now
Your purpose is to fright me—a troubadour
You play with words. You had never used so
    many,
Not if you meant it, I am sure. The child . . .
No . . . mercy! No!   [*Kneels.*

Eleanor. Play! . . . that bosom never
Heaved under the King's hand with such true
    passion
As at this loveless knife that stirs the riot,
Which it will quench in blood! Slave, if he love
    thee,
Thy life is worth the wrestle for it: arise,
And dash thyself against me that I may slay
    thee!
The worm! shall I let her go? But ha! what's
    here?
By very God, the cross I gave the King!
His village darling in some lewd caress
Has wheedled it off the King's neck to her
    own.
By thy leave, beauty. Ay, the same! I warrant
Thou hast sworn on this my cross a hundred
    times
Never to leave him—and that merits death,
False oath on holy cross—for thou must leave
    him
To-day, but not quite yet. My good Fitzurse,
The running down the chase is kindlier sport
Ev'n than the death. Who knows but that thy
    lover
May plead so pitifully, that I may spare
    thee?
Come hither, man; stand there. (*To Rosamund.*)
    Take thy one chance;

Catch at the last straw. Kneel to thy lord
    Fitzurse ;
Crouch even because thou hatest him ; fawn
    upon him
For thy life and thy son's.
    Rosamund (rising).   I am a Clifford,
My son a Clifford and Plantagenet.
I am to die then, tho' there stand beside thee
One who might grapple with thy dagger, if he
Had aught of man, or thou of woman ; or I
Would bow to such a baseness as would make
    me
Most worthy of it : both of us will die,
And I will fly with my sweet boy to heaven,
And shriek to all the saints among the stars :
" Eleanor of Aquitaine, Eleanor of England !
Murder'd by the adulteress Eleanor,
Whose doings are a horror to the east,
A hissing in the west ! "   Have we not heard
Raymond of Poitou, thine own uncle—nay,
Geoffrey Plantagenet, thine own husband's
    father—
Nay, ev'n the accursed heathen Saladdeen—
Strike !
I challenge thee to meet me before God.
Answer me there.
    Eleanor (raising the dagger).   This in thy
    bosom, fool,
And after in thy bastard's !

Enter BECKET *from behind. Catches hold of her arm.*

Becket. Murderess!
[*The dagger falls ; they stare at one another. After a pause.*
Eleanor. My lord, we know you proud of your fine hand,
But having now admired it long enough,
We find that it is mightier than it seems—
At least mine own is frailer : you are laming it.
Becket. And lamed and maim'd to dislocation, better
Than raised to take a life which Henry bade me
Guard from the stroke that dooms thee after death
To wail in deathless flame.
Eleanor. Nor you, nor I
Have now to learn, my lord, that our good Henry
Says many a thing in sudden heats, which he
Gainsays by next sunrising—often ready
To tear himself for having said as much
My lord, Fitzurse—
Becket. He too ! what dost thou here?
Dares the bear slouch into the lion's den ?
One downward plunge of his paw would rend away
Eyesight and manhood, life itself, from thee.

Go, lest I blast thee with anathema,
And make thee a world's horror.
    Fitzurse.   My lord, I shall
Remember this.
    Becket.   I *do* remember thee ;
Lest I remember thee to the lion, go.
                        [*Exit* FITZURSE.
Take up your dagger ; put it in the sheath.
    Eleanor. Might not your courtesy stoop to
        hand it me ?
But crowns must bow when mitres sit so high.
Well—well—too costly to be left or lost.
                  [*Picks up the dagger.*
I had it from an Arab soldan, who,
When I was there in Antioch, marvell'd at
Our unfamiliar beauties of the west ;
But wonder'd more at my much constancy
To the monk-king, Louis, our former burden,
From whom, as being too kin, you know, my
        lord,
God's grace and Holy Church deliver'd us.
I think, time given, I could have talk'd him
        out of
His ten wives into one. Look at the hilt.
What excellent workmanship. In our poor west
We cannot do it so well.
    Becket.   We can do worse.
Madam, I saw your dagger at her throat ;
I heard your savage cry.

Eleanor.   Well acted, was it?
A comedy meant to seem a tragedy—
A feint, a farce. My honest lord, you are known
Thro' all the courts of Christendom as one
That mars a cause with over-violence.
You have wrong'd Fitzurse. I speak not of my-
    self.
We thought to scare this minion of the King
Back from her churchless commerce with the
    King
To the fond arms of her first love, Fitzurse,
Who swore to marry her. You have spoilt the
    farce.
My savage cry? Why, she—she—when I strove
To work against her license for her good,
Bark'd out at me such monstrous charges, that
The King himself, for love of his own sons,
If hearing, would have spurn'd her; whereupon
I menaced her with this, as when we threaten
A yelper with a stick. Nay, I deny not
That I was somewhat anger'd. Do you hear me?
Believe or no, I care not. You have lost
The ear of the King. I have it. . . . My Lord
    Paramount,
Our great High-priest, will not your Holiness
Vouchsafe a gracious answer to your Queen?
    Becket. Rosamund hath not answer'd you one
    word;
Madam, I will not answer you one word.

Daughter, the world hath trick'd thee.   Leave it,
      daughter,
Come thou with me to Godstow nunnery,
And live what may be left thee of a life
Saved as by miracle alone with Him
Who gave it.

Reënter GEOFFREY.

Geoffrey. Mother, you told me a great fib: it
      wasn't in the willow.
Becket. Follow us, my son, and we will find it
      for thee—
Or something manlier.

> [*Exeunt* BECKET ROSAMUND *and*
>   GEOFFREY.

Eleanor. The world hath trick'd her—that's the
      King ; if so,
There was the farce, the feint—not mine.   And
      yet
I am all but sure my dagger was a feint
Till the worm turn'd—not life shot up in blood,
But death drawn in ;—(*looking at the vial*) *this*
      was no feint then ? no.
But can I swear to that, had she but given
Plain answer to plain query ? nay, methinks
Had she but bow'd herself to meet the wave
Of humiliation, worshipt whom she loathed
I should have let her be, scorn'd her too much
To harm her.   Henry—Becket tells him this—

To take my life might lose him Aquitaine.
Too politic for that. Imprison me?
No, for it came to nothing—only a feint.
Did she not tell me I was playing on her?
I'll swear to mine own self it
    was a feint.
Why should I swear, Eleanor,
    who am, or was,
A sovereign power? The
    King plucks out their
    eyes
Who anger him, and shall not
    I, the Queen,
Tear out her heart—kill, kill
    with knife or venom
One of his slanderous harlots?
    "None of such?"
I love her none the more.
    Tut, the chance gone,
She lives—but not for him;
    one point is gain'd.
O I, that thro' the Pope di-
    vorced King Louis,
Scorning his monkery,—I that
    wedded Henry,
Honoring his manhood—will he not mock at me
The jealous fool balk'd of her will—with *him?*
But he and he must never meet again.
Reginald Fitzurse '

Reënter FITZURSE.

Fitzurse.   Here, Madam, at your pleasure.
Eleanor.   My pleasure is to have a man about
     me.
Why did you slink away so like a cur?
Fitzurse.   Madam, I am as much man as the
     King.
Madam, I fear Church-censures like your King.
Eleanor.   He grovels to the Church when he's
     black-blooded,
But kinglike fought the proud archbishop,—king-
     like
Defied the Pope, and, like his kingly sires,
The Normans, striving still to break or bind
The spiritual giant with our island laws
And customs, made me for the moment proud
Ev'n of that stale Church-bond which link'd me
     with him
To bear him kingly sons.   I am not so sure
But that I love him still.   Thou as much man!
No more of that; we will to France and be
Beforehand with the King, and brew from out
This Godstow-Becket intermeddling such
A strong hate-philtre as may madden him—madden
Against his priest beyond all hellebore.

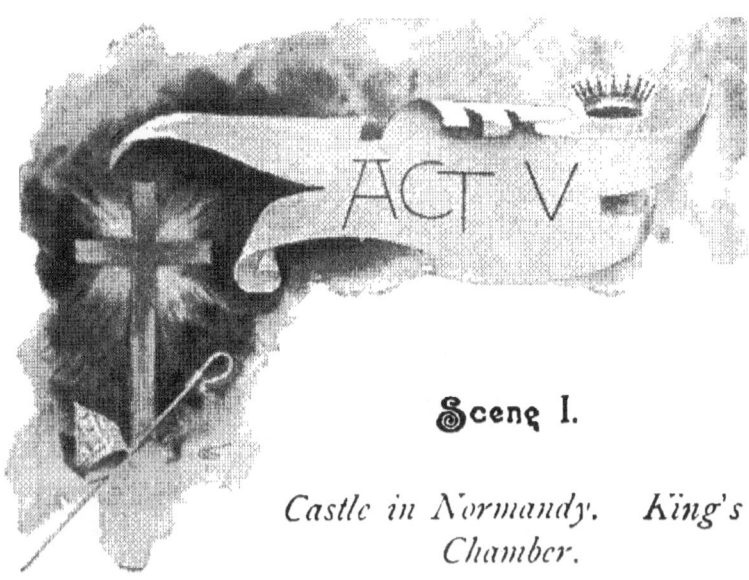

Scene I.

Castle in Normandy. King's Chamber.

HENRY, ROGER OF YORK, FOLIOT, JOCELYN OF SALISBURY.

Roger of York. Nay, nay, my liege,
He rides abroad with armed followers,
Hath broken all his promises to thyself,
Cursed and anathematized us right and left,
Stirr'd up a party there against your son—
Henry. Roger of York, you always hated him,
Even when you both were boys at Theobald's.
Roger of York. I always hated boundless arro-
gance.
In mine own cause I strove against him there,
And in thy cause I strive against him now.

Henry.   I cannot think he moves against my
     son,
Knowing right well with what a tenderness
He loved my son.
     Roger of York.   Before you made him king.
But Becket ever moves against a king.
The Church is all—the crime to be a king.
We   trust   your   Royal   Grace,   lord   of   more
     land
Than any crown in Europe, will not yield
To lay your neck beneath your citizen's heel.
     Henry.   Not   to   a   Gregory   of   my   throning!
     No.
Foliot.   My royal liege, in aiming at your love,
It may be sometimes I have overshot
My duties to our Holy Mother Church,
Tho' all the world allows I fall no inch
Behind this Becket, rather go beyond
In scourgings, macerations, mortifyings,
Fasts, disciplines that clear the spiritual eye,
And   break   the   soul   from   earth.   Let   all   that
     be.
I boast not: but you know thro' all this quarrel
I   still   have   cleaved   to   the   crown,   in   hope   the
     crown
Would   cleave   to   me   that   but   obey'd   the
     crown,
Crowning   your   son;   for   which   our   loyal
     service,

And since we likewise swore to obey the
    customs,
York and myself, and our good Salisbury
    here,
Are push'd from out communion of the Church.
    Jocelyn of Salisbury. Becket hath trodden on
    us like worms, my liege ;
Trodden one half dead ; one half, but half alive,
Cries to the King.
    Henry (aside). Take care o' thyself, O King.
    Jocelyn of Salisbury. Being so crush'd and so
    humiliated
We scarcely dare to bless the food we eat
Because of Becket.
    Henry.   What would ye have me do ?
    Roger of York. Summon your barons ; take
    their counsel : yet
I know — could swear — as long as Becket
    breathes,
Your Grace will never have one quiet hour.
    Henry. What ? . . . Ay . . . but pray
    you do not work upon me.
I see your drift . . . it may be so . . . and yet
You know me easily anger'd. Will you hence ?
He shall absolve you . . . you shall have redress.
I have a dizzying headache. Let me rest.
I'll call you by and by.
            [*Exeunt* ROGER OF YORK, FOLIOT,
                and JOCELYN OF SALISBURY.

Would he were dead! I have lost all love for
    him.
If God would take him in some sudden way—

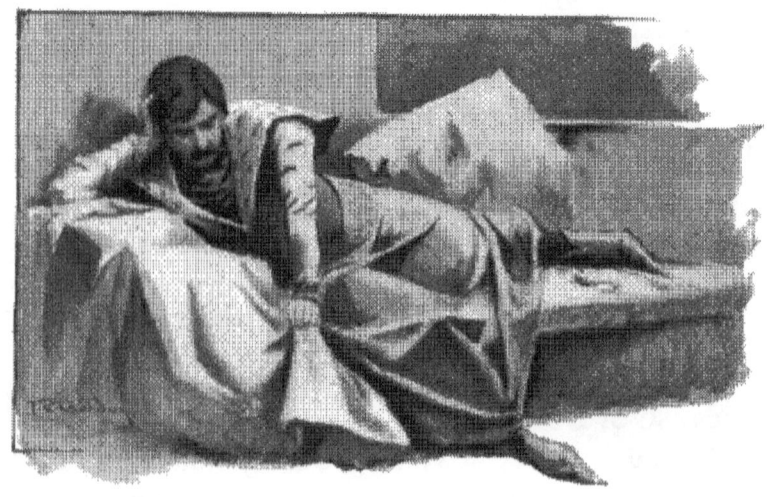

Would he were dead.   *[Lies down.*
    Page (entering). My liege, the Queen of Eng-
    land.
    Henry. God's eyes!   *[Starting up.*

           Enter ELEANOR.

    Eleanor.   Of England? Say of Aquitaine.
I am no Queen of England. I had dream'd
I was the bride of England, and a queen.
    Henry. And,—while you dream'd you were
    the bride of England,—
Stirring her baby-king against me? ha!

Eleanor. The brideless Becket is thy king and
    mine :
I will go live and die in Aquitaine.
    Henry. Except I clap thee into prison here,
Lest thou shouldst play the wanton there again.
Ha, you of Aquitaine ! O you of Aquitaine !
You were but Aquitaine to Louis—no wife ;
You are only Aquitaine to me—no wife.
    Eleanor. And why, my lord, should I be wife
    to one
That only wedded me for Aquitaine ?
Yet this no wife—her six and thirty sail
Of Provence blew you to your English throne ;
And this no wife has borne you four brave
    sons,
And one of them at least is like to prove
Bigger in our small world than thou art.
    Henry.   Ay—
Richard, if he *be* mine—I hope him mine.
But thou art like enough to make him thine.
    Eleanor. Becket is like enough to make all
    his.
    Henry. Methought I had recover'd of the
    Becket,
That all was planed and bevell'd smooth again,
Save from some hateful cantrip of thine own.
    Eleanor. I will go live and die in Aquitaine.
I dream'd I was the consort of a king,
Not one whose back his priest has broken.

Henry.   What !
Is the end come ?   You, will you crown my foe
My victor in mid-battle ?   I will be
Sole master of my house.   The end is mine.
What game, what juggle, what devilry are you
     playing ?
Why do you thrust this Becket on me again ?
    Eleanor.   Why ? for I *am* true wife, and have
     my fears
Lest Becket thrust you even from your throne.
Do you know this cross, my liege ?
    Henry (*turning his head*).   Away ! not I.
    Eleanor.   Not ev'n the central diamond, worth,
     I think,
Half of the Antioch whence I had it ?
    Henry.   That ?
    Eleanor.   I gave it you, and you your para-
     mour ;
She sends it back, as being dead to earth,
So dead henceforth to you.
    Henry.   Dead ! you have murder'd her.
Found out her secret bower and murder'd her.
    Eleanor.   Your Becket knew the secret of
     your bower.
    Henry (*calling out*).   Ho there ! thy rest of
     life is hopeless prison.
    Eleanor.   And what would my own Aquitaine
     say to that ?
First free thy captive from *her* hopeless prison.

Henry. O devil, can I free her from the
    grave?

Eleanor. You are too tragic : both of us are
    players
In such a comedy as our court of Provence
Had laugh'd at. That's a delicate Latin lay
Of Walter Map : the lady holds the cleric
Lovelier than any soldier, his poor tonsure
A crown of Empire. Will you have it again?
    (*Offering the cross. He dashes it down.*)
St. Cupid, that is too irreverent.
Then mine once more. (*Puts it on.*)
                Your cleric hath your lady.
Nay, what uncomely faces, could he see you !
Foam at the mouth because King Thomas,
    lord
Not only of your vassals but amours,
Thro' chastest honor of the Decalogue,
Hath used the full authority of his Church
To put her into Godstow nunnery.

Henry. To put her into Godstow nunnery !
He dared not—liar ! yet, yet I remember—
I do remember.
He bade me put her into a nunnery—
Into Godstow, into Hellstow, Devilstow !
The Church ! the Church !
God's eyes ! I would the Church were down in
    hell !   [*Exit.*

Eleanor. Aha !

Enter the four KNIGHTS.

Fitzurse.   What made the King cry out so
   furiously ?
Eleanor.   Our Becket, who will not absolve
   the Bishops.
I think ye four have cause to love this Becket.
   Fitzurse.   I hate him for his insolence to all.
   De Tracy.   And I for all his insolence to thee.
   De Brito.   I hate him for I hate him is my
   reason,
And yet I hate him for a hypocrite.
   De Morville.   I do not love him, for he did his
   best
To break the barons, and now braves the King.
   Eleanor.   Strike, then, at once ; the King
   would have him—See !

Reënter HENRY.

Henry.   No man to love me, honor me, obey
   me !
Sluggards and fools !
The slave that eat my bread has kick'd his King !
The dog I crammed with dainties worried me !
The fellow that on a lame jade came to court,
A ragged cloak for saddle—he, he, he,
To shake my throne, to push into my chamber—
My bed, where ev'n the slave is private—he—

I'll have her out again, he shall absolve
The Bishops—they but did my will—not you—
Sluggards and fools, why do you stand and stare?
You are no king's men—you—you—you are
    Becket's men.
Down with King Henry! up with the Arch-
    bishop!
Will no man rid me from this pestilent priest?
                                    [*Exit.*
            [*The* KNIGHTS *draw their swords.*
Eleanor. *Are* ye king's men? I am king's
    woman, I.
The Knights. King's men! King's men!

Scene II.

A Room in Canterbury Monastery.

BECKET *and* JOHN OF SALISBURY.

Becket.   York said so?
    John of Salisbury.   Yes : a man may
       take good counsel
Ev'n from his foe.
    Becket.   York will say anything.
What is he saying now? gone to the King
And taken our anathema with him.   York!
Can the King de-anathematize this York?
    John of Salisbury.   Thomas, I would thou
       hadst return'd to England,
Like some wise prince of this world from his wars,
With more of olive-branch and amnesty
For foes at home—thou hast raised the world
       against thee.
    Becket.   Why, John, my kingdom is not of this
       world.
    John of Salisbury.   If it were more of this
       world it might be
More of the next.   A policy of wise pardon
Wins here as well as there.   To bless thine
       enemies—

Becket. Ay, mine, not Heaven's.

John of Salisbury. And may there not be
    something
Of this world's leaven in thee too, when crying
On Holy Church to thunder out her rights
And thine own wrong so pitilessly.   Ah,
    Thomas,
The lightnings that we think are only Heaven's
Flash sometimes out of earth against the heavens.
The soldier, when he lets his whole self go
Lost in the common good, the common wrong,
Strikes truest ev'n for his own self.   I crave
Thy pardon—I have still thy leave to speak.
Thou hast waged God's war against the King;
    and yet
We are self-uncertain creatures, and we may,
Yea, even when we know not, mix our spites
And private hates with our defence of Heaven.

Enter EDWARD GRIM.

Becket. Thou art but yesterday from Cam-
    bridge, Grim;
What say ye there of Becket?
    Grim.   *I* believe him
The bravest in our roll of Primates down
From Austin—there are some—for there are
    men
Of canker'd judgment everywhere—

Becket.   Who hold
With York, with York against me.
  Grim.   Well, my lord,
A stranger monk desires access to you.
  Becket. York against Canterbury, York against
    God !
I am open to him.   [*Exit* GRIM.

Enter ROSAMUND *as a Monk.*

Rosamund.   Can I speak with you
Alone, my father ?
  Becket.   Come you to confess ?
  Rosamund. Not now.
  Becket. Then speak ; this is my other self,
Who like my conscience never lets me be.
  Rosamund (*throwing back the cowl*). I know
    him ; our good John of Salisbury.
  Becket. Breaking already from thy novitiate
To plunge into this bitter world again—
These wells of Marah. I am grieved, my
    daughter.
I thought that I had made a peace for thee.
  Rosamund. Small peace was mine in my no-
    vitiate, father.
Thro' all closed doors a dreadful whisper crept
That thou wouldst excommunicate the King.
I could not eat, sleep, pray : I had with me

The monk's disguise thou gavest me for my
    bower :
I think our Abbess knew it and allow'd it.
I fled, and found thy name a charm to get me
Food, roof, and rest.   I met a robber once,
I told him I was bound to see the Archbishop ;
" Pass on," he said, and in thy name I pass'd
From house to house. In one a son stone-
    blind
Sat by his mother's hearth : he had gone too far
Into the King's own woods ; and the poor
    mother,
Soon as she learnt I was a friend of thine,
Cried out against the cruelty of the King.
I said it was the King's courts, not the King ;
But she would not believe me, and she wish'd
The Church were king : she had seen the Arch-
    bishop once,
So mild, so kind. The people love thee, father.
    Becket. Alas ! when I was Chancellor to the
    King,
I fear I was as cruel as the King.
    Rosamund. Cruel ? Oh, no—it is the law, not
    he ;
The customs of the realm.
    Becket.   The customs ! customs !
    Rosamund. My lord, you have not excommu-
    nicated him ?
Oh, if you have, absolve him !

Becket.   Daughter, daughter,
Deal not with things you know not.
    Rosamund.   I know *him*.
Then you have done it, and I call *you* cruel.
    John of Salisbury.   No, daughter, you mistake
      our good Archbishop ;
For once in France the King had been so
      harsh,
He thought to excommunicate him—Thomas,
You could not—old affection master'd you,
You falter'd into tears.
    Rosamund.   God bless him for it.
    Becket.   Nay, make me not a woman, John of
      Salisbury,
Nor make me traitor to my holy office.
Did not a man's voice ring along the aisle,
" The King is sick and almost unto death."
How could I excommunicate him then ?
    Rosamund.   And wilt thou excommunicate him
      now ?
    Becket.   Daughter, my time is short.   I shall
      not do it.
And were it longer—well—I should not do it.
    Rosamund.   Thanks in this life, and in the life
      to come.
    Becket.   Get thee back to thy nunnery with
      all haste ;
Let this be thy last trespass.   But one ques-
      tion—

How fares thy pretty boy, the little Geoffrey?
No fever, cough, croup, sickness?
   Rosamund.   No, but saved
From all that by our solitude.   The plagues
That smite the city spare the solitudes.
   Becket.   God save him from all sickness of the
      soul!
Thee too, thy solitude among thy nuns,
May that save thee!   Doth he remember me?
   Rosamund.   I warrant him.
   Becket.   He is marvellously like thee.
   Rosamund.   Liker the King.
   Becket.   No, daughter.
   Rosamund.   Ay, but wait
Till his nose rises; he will be very king.
   Becket.   Ev'n so: but think not of the King:
      farewell!
   Rosamund.   My lord, the city is full of armed
      men.
   Becket.   Ev'n so: farewell!
   Rosamund.   I will but pass to vespers,
And breathe one prayer for my liege-lord the
      King,
His child and mine own soul, and so return.
   Becket.   Pray for me too: much need of
      prayer have I.
                [ROSAMUND *kneels and goes.*
Dan John, how much we lose, we celibates,
Lacking the love of woman and of child.

John of Salisbury.   More gain than loss; for
   of your wives you shall
Find one a slut whose fairest linen seems
Foul as her dust-cloth, if she used it—one
            So charged with tongue, that
               every thread of thought
                  Is broken ere it
                     joins—a
                     shrew to
                     boot,

Whose evil song far on into the night
Thrills to the topmost tile—no hope but death;
One slow, fat, white, a burden of the hearth;
And one that being thwarted ever swoons
And weeps herself into the place of power;
And one an *uxor pauperis Ibyci.*

So rare the household honeymaking bee,
Man's help! but we, we have the Blessed Virgin
For worship, and our Mother Church for bride ;
And all the souls we saved and father'd here
Will greet us as our babes in Paradise.
What noise was that? she told us of arm'd
    men
Here in the city.   Will you not withdraw?
  Becket.   I once was out with Henry in the
    days
When Henry loved me, and we came upon
A wild-fowl sitting on her nest, so still
I reach'd my hand and touch'd ; she did not
    stir ;
The snow had frozen round her, and she sat
Stone-dead upon a heap of ice-cold eggs. .
Look ! how this love, this mother, runs thro' all
The world God made—even the beast—the
    bird !
  John of Salisbury.   Ay, still a lover of the
    beast and bird ?
But these arm'd men—will you not hide yourself?
Perchance the fierce De Brocs from Saltwood
    Castle,
To assail our Holy Mother lest she brood
Too long o'er this hard egg, the world, and
    send
Her whole heart's heat into it, till it break
Into young angels.   Pray you, hide yourself.

Becket. There was a little fair-hair'd Norman maid
Lived in my mother's house: if Rosamund is
The world's rose, as her name imports her—she
Was the world's lily.
 John of Salisbury. Ay, and what of her?
 Becket. She died of leprosy.
 John of Salisbury.   I know not why
You call these old things back again, my lord.
 Becket. The drowning man, they say, remembers all
The chances of his life, just ere he dies.
 John of Salisbury. Ay—but these arm'd men
 —will *you* drown *yourself?*
He loses half the meed of martyrdom
Who will be martyr when he might escape.
 Becket. What day of the week? Tuesday?
 John of Salisbury. Tuesday, my lord.
 Becket. On a Tuesday was I born, and on a Tuesday
Baptized; and on a Tuesday did I fly
Forth from Northampton; on a Tuesday pass'd
From England into bitter banishment;
On a Tuesday at Pontigny came to me
The ghostly warning of my martyrdom;

On a Tuesday from mine exile I return'd,
And on a Tuesday—

[TRACY *enters, then* FITZURSE, DE BRITO, *and*
DE MORVILLE. MONKS *following*.

                      —on a Tuesday—Tracy!

A long silence broken by FITZURSE *saying, con-*
temptuously,

God help thee!
   John of Salisbury (*aside*).   How the good
     Archbishop reddens!
He never yet could brook the note of scorn.
   Fitzurse.   My lord, we bring a message from
     the King
Beyond the water; will you have it alone,
Or with these listeners near you?
   Becket.   As you will.
   Fitzurse.   Nay, as *you* will.
   Becket.   Nay, as *you* will.
   John of Salisbury.   Why then
Better perhaps to speak with them apart.
Let us withdraw.

[*All go out except the four* KNIGHTS *and*
BECKET.

   Fitzurse.   We are all alone with him.
Shall I not smite him with his own cross-staff?

De Morville.   No, look ! the door is open : let
   him be.

Fitzurse.   The King condemns your excom-
   municating—

Becket.   This is no secret, but a public matter.
In here again !

[JOHN OF SALISBURY *and* MONKS *return.*

Now, sirs, the King's commands !

Fitzurse.   The King beyond the water, thro'
   our voices,
Commands you to be dutiful and leal
To your young King on this side of the water,
Not scorn him for the foibles of his youth.
What ! you would make his coronation void
By cursing those who crown'd him.   Out upon
   you !

Becket.   Reginald, all men know I loved the
   Prince.
His father gave him to my care, and I
Became his second father : he had his faults,
For which I would have laid mine own life down
To help him from them, since indeed I loved
   him,
And love him next after my lord his father.
Rather than dim the splendor of his crown
I fain would treble and quadruple it
With revenues, realms, and golden provinces
So that were done in equity.

Fitzurse.   You have broken
Your bond of peace, your treaty with the King—
Wakening such brawls and loud disturbances
In England, that he calls you oversea
To answer for it in his Norman courts.
    Becket. Prate not of bonds, for never, oh, never
        again
Shall the waste voice of the bond-breaking sea
Divide me from the mother church of England,
My Canterbury. Loud disturbances!
Oh, ay—the bells rang out even to deafening,
Organ and pipe, and dulcimer, chants and hymns
In all the churches, trumpets in the halls,
Sobs, laughter, cries: they spread their raiment
        down
Before me—would have made my pathway flow-
        ers,
Save that it was mid-winter in the street,
But full mid-summer in those honest hearts.
    Fitzurse. The King commands you to absolve
        the bishops
Whom you have excommunicated.
    Becket. I? Not I, the Pope. Ask *him* for
        absolution.
    Fitzurse. But you advised the Pope.
    Becket.   And so I did.
They have but to submit.
    The Four Knights. The King commands you.
We are all King's men.

Becket.　King's men at least should know
That their own King closed with me last July
That I should pass the censures of the Church
On those that crown'd young Henry in this realm,
And trampled on the rights of Canterbury.
　　Fitzurse.　What! dare you charge the King
　　　with treachery?
He sanction thee to excommunicate
The prelates whom he chose to crown his son!
　　Becket.　I spake no word of treachery, Reginald.
But for the truth of this I make appeal
To all the archbishops, bishops, prelates, barons,
Monks, knights, five hundred, that were there
　　　and heard.
Nay, you yourself were there: you heard your-
　　　self.
　　Fitzurse.　I was not there.
　　Becket.　　　　　　　　I saw you there.
　　Fitzurse.　　　　　　　　　　　I was not.
　　Becket.　You were.　I never forget anything.
　　Fitzurse.　He makes the King a traitor, me a
　　　liar.
How long shall we forbear him?
　　John of Salisbury (drawing BECKET *aside).*　O
　　　my good lord,
Speak with them privately on this hereafter.
You see they have been revelling, and I fear
Are braced and brazen'd up with Christmas wines
For any murderous brawl.

Becket.   And yet they prate
Of mine, my brawls, when those, that name them-
    selves
Of the King's part, have broken down our
    barns,
Wasted out diocese, outraged our tenants,
Lifted our produce, driven our clerics out—
Why they, your friends, those ruffians, the De
    Brocs,
They stood on Dover beach to murder me,
They slew my stags in mine own manor here,
Mutilated, poor brute, my sumpter-mule,
Plunder'd the vessel full of Gascon wine,
The old King's present, carried off the casks,
Kill'd half the crew, dungeon'd the other half
In Pevensey Castle—
    De Morville.   Why not rather then,
If this be so, complain to your young King,
Not punish of your own authority?
    Becket.   Mine enemies barr'd all access to the
    boy.
They knew he loved me.
Hugh, Hugh, how proudly you exalt your
    head!
Nay, when they seek to overturn our rights,
I ask no leave of king, or mortal man,
To set them straight again.   Alone I do it.
Give to the King the things that are the King's,
And those of God to God.

Fitzurse.   Threats! threats! ye hear him.
What! will he excommunicate all the world?
                    [*The* KNIGHTS *come round* BECKET.
De Tracy.   He shall not.
De Brito.   Well, as yet—I should be grate-
      ful—
He hath not excommunicated *me.*
      Becket.   Because thou wast *born* excommuni-
      cate.
I never spied in thee one gleam of grace.
      De Brito.   Your Christian's Christian charity!
      Becket.   By St. Denis—
      De Brito.   Ay, by St. Denis, now will he flame
      out,
And lose his head as old St. Denis did.
      Becket.   Ye think to scare me from my loyalty
To God and to the Holy Father.   No!
Tho' all the swords in England flashed above
      me
Ready to fall at Henry's word or yours—
Tho' all the loud-lung'd trumpets upon earth
Blared from the heights of all the thrones of her
      kings,
Blowing the world against me, I would stand
Clothed with the full authority of Rome,
Mail'd in the perfect panoply of faith,
First of the foremost of their files, who die
For God, to people heaven in the great day
When God makes up his jewels.   Once I fled—

Never again, and you—I marvel at you—
Ye know what is between us. Ye have sworn
Yourselves my men when I was Chancellor—
My vassals—and yet threaten your Archbishop
In his own house.

    Knights.   Nothing can be between us
That goes against our fealty to the King.

    Fitzurse. And in his name we charge you that
       ye keep
This traitor from escaping.

    Becket.   Rest you easy,
For I am easy to keep.   I shall not fly.
Here, here, here will you find me.

    De Morville.   Know you not
You have spoken to the peril of your life?

    Becket. As I shall speak again.

    Fitzurse, De Tracy, and De Brito. To arms !

        [*They rush out,* DE MORVILLE *lingers.*

    Becket.   De Morville,
I had thought so well of you ; and even now
You seem the least assassin of the four.
Oh, do not damn yourself for company !
Is it too late for me to save your soul ?
I pray you for one moment stay and speak.

    De Morville. Becket, it *is* too late.   [*Exit.*

    Becket.   Is it too late ?
Too late on earth may be too soon in hell.

    Knights (*in the distance*). Close the great gate
      —ho, there—upon the town.

Becket's Retainers.   Shut the hall-doors.

[*A pause.*

Becket.   You hear them, brother John ;
Why do you stand so silent, brother John ?

John of Salisbury.   For I was musing on an
ancient saw,
Suaviter in modo, fortiter in re,
Is strength less strong when hand-in-hand with
grace ?
Gratior in pulchro corpore virtus.   Thomas,
Why should you heat yourself for such as
these ?

Becket.   Methought I answer'd moderately
enough.

John of Salisbury.   As one that blows the
coal to cool the fire.
My lord, I marvel why you never lean
On any man's advising but your own.

Becket.   Is it so, Dan John ? well, what should
I have done ?

John of Salisbury.   You should have taken
counsel with your friends
Before these bandits brake into your presence.
They seek—you make—occasion for your death.

Becket.   My counsel is already taken, John.
I am prepared to die.

John of Salisbury.   We are sinners all,
The best of all not all-prepared to die.

Becket.   God's will be done !

John of Salisbury. Ay, well. God's will be
  done!
Grim (reëntering). My lord, the knights are
  arming in the garden
Beneath the sycamore.
  Becket.   Good! let them arm.
Grim. And one of the De Brocs is with them,
  Robert,
The apostate monk that was with Randulf here.
He knows the twists and turnings of the place.
  Becket. No fear!
Grim.   No fear, my lord.
    [*Crashes on the hall-doors. The* MONKS *flee.*
Becket (rising).   Our dovecote flown!
I cannot tell why monks should all be cowards.
  John of Salisbury. Take refuge in your own
    cathedral, Thomas.
  Becket. Do they not fight the Great Fiend day
    by day?
Valor and holy life should go together.
Why should all monks be cowards?
  John of Salisbury.   Are they so?
I say, take refuge in your own cathedral.
  Becket. Ay, but I told them I would wait them
    here.
  Grim. May they not say you dared not show
    yourself
In your old place? and vespers are beginning.
    [*Bell rings for vespers till end of scene.*

You should attend the office, give them heart.
They fear you slain : they dread they know not
    what.

   Becket.   Ay, monks, not men.

   Grim.   I am a monk, my lord.
Perhaps, my lord, you wrong us.
Some would stand by you to the death.

   Becket.   Your pardon.

   John of Salisbury.   He said "Attend the
    office."

   Becket.   Attend the office ?
Why then—The Cross !—who bears my Cross
    before me ?
Methought they would have brain'd me with it,
    John.   [GRIM *takes it.*

   Grim.   I ! Would that I could bear thy cross
    indeed !

   Becket.   The Mitre !

   John of Salisbury.   Will you wear it ?—
    there !   [BECKET *puts on the mitre.*

   Becket.   The Pall !
I go to meet my King !   [*Puts on the pall.*

   Grim.   To meet the King ?
        [*Crashes on the doors as they go out.*

   John of Salisbury.   Why do you move with
    such a stateliness ?
Can you not hear them yonder like a storm,
Battering the doors, and breaking thro' the
    walls ?

Becket. Why do the heathen rage? My two
    good friends,
What matters murder'd here, or murder'd there?
And yet my dream foretold my martyrdom
In mine own church. It is God's will. Go on.
Nay, drag me not. We must not seem to fly.

Scene III.

North Transept of Canterbury Cathedral.

On the right hand a flight of steps leading to the Choir, another flight on the left, leading to the North Aisle. Winter afternoon slowly darkening. Low thunder now and then of an approaching storm. MONKS *heard chanting the service.* ROSAMUND *kneeling.*

Rosamund. O blessed saint, O glorious
           Benedict,—
    These arm'd men in the city, these
    fierce faces—
Thy holy follower founded Canterbury—
Save that dear head which now is Canter-
    bury,
Save him, he saved my life, he saved my
    child,
Save him, his blood would darken Henry's
    name ;
Save him till all as saintly as thyself
He miss the searching flame of purgatory,
And pass at once perfect to Paradise.
       [Noise of steps and voices in the cloisters.
Hark ! Is it they ? Coming ! He is not here—
Not yet, thank Heaven. O save him !
       [Goes up steps leading to choir.

Becket (*entering, forced along by* JOHN OF SALIS-
BURY *and* GRIM). No, I tell you!
I cannot bear a hand upon my person,
Why do you force me thus against my will?
   Grim. My lord, we force you from your
     enemies.
   Becket. As you would force a king from being
     crown'd.
   John of Salisbury. We must not force the
     crown of martyrdom.
         [*Service stops.* MONKS *come down from
          the stairs that lead to the choir.*
   Monks. Here is the great Archbishop! He
     lives! he lives!
Die with him, and be glorified together.
   Becket. Together? . . . get you back! go on
     with the office.
   Monks. Come, then, with us to vespers.
   Becket.   How can I come
When you so block the entry? Back, I say!
Go on with the office. Shall not Heaven be
     served
Tho' earth's last earthquake clash'd the minster-
     bells,
And the great deeps were broken up again,
And hiss'd against the sun?
             [*Noise in the cloisters.*
   Monks.   The murderers, hark!
Let us hide! let us hide!

Becket.   What do these people fear?
Monks.   Those arm'd men in the cloister.
Becket.   Be not such cravens!
I will go out and meet them.
Grim and others.   Shut the doors!
We will not have him slain before our face.
   [*They close the doors of the transept. Knocking.*
Fly, fly, my lord, before they burst the doors!
                              [*Knocking.*
   Becket.   Why, these are our own monks who
        follow'd us!
And will you bolt them out, and have *them* slain?
Undo the doors: the church is not a castle:
Knock, and it shall be open'd.   Are you deaf?
What, have I lost authority among you?
Stand by, make way!

   [*Opens the doors.   Enter* MONKS *from cloister.*

                    Come in, my friends, come in!
Nay, faster, faster!
   Monks.   Oh, my lord Archbishop,
A score of knights all arm'd with swords and
        axes—
To the choir, to the choir!

      [MONKS *divide, part flying by the stairs on the
      right, part by those on the left.   The rush
      of these last bears* BECKET *along with them
      some way up the steps, where he is left stand-
      ing alone.*

Becket.　　　　　Shall I too pass to the choir
And die upon the patriarchal throne
Of all my predecessors?
　John of Salisbury.　　　No, to the crypt!
Twenty steps down. Stumble not in the dark-
　　　ness,
Lest they should seize thee.
　Grim.　　　　　To the crypt? no—no,
To the chapel of St. Blaise beneath the roof!
　*John of Salisbury (pointing upward and down-
　　　ward).* That way, or this! Save thyself
　　　either way.
　Becket. Oh, no, not either way, nor any way,
Save by that way which leads thro' night to light.
Not twenty steps, but one.
And fear not I should stumble in the darkness,
Not tho' it be their hour, the power of darkness,
But my hour too, the power of light in darkness!
I am not in the darkness but the light,
Seen by the Church in Heaven, the Church on
　　　earth—
The power of life in death to make her free!

　[*Enter the four* KNIGHTS. JOHN OF SALISBURY
　　flies to the altar of St. Benedict.

　Fitzurse. Here, here, King's men!
　　　[*Catches hold of the last flying* MONK.
　　　Where is the traitor Becket?

Monk. I am not he ! I am not he, my lord.
I am not he indeed !

   Fitzurse.   Hence to the fiend !

                             [*Pushes him away.*

Where is this treble traitor to the King ?

   De Tracy. Where is the Archbishop, Thomas
     Becket ?

   Becket.   Here.

No traitor to the King, but Priest of God,
Primate of England. [*Descending into the transept.*

                     I am he ye seek.

What would ye have of me ?

   Fitzurse.   Your life.

   De Tracy.   Your life.

   De Morville. Save that you will absolve the
     bishops.

   Becket.   Never,—

Except they make submission to the Church.
You had my answer to that cry before.

   De Morville. Why, then you are a dead man ;
     flee !

   Becket. I will not.

I am readier to be slain, than thou to slay.
Hugh, I know well thou hast but half a heart
To bathe this sacred pavement with my blood.
God pardon thee and these, but God's full
     curse
Shatter you all to pieces if ye harm
One of my flock !

Fitzurse. Was not the great gate shut?
They are thronging in to vespers—half the town.
We shall be overwhelm'd. Seize him and carry
    him!
Come with us—nay—thou art our prisoner—
    come!

De Morville. Ay, make him prisoner, do not
    harm the man.
            [FITZURSE *lays hold of the* ARCH-
                BISHOP'S *pall.*

Becket. Touch me not!

De Brito. How the good priest gods himself!
He is not yet ascended to the Father.

Fitzurse. I will not only touch, but drag thee
    hence.

Becket. Thou art my man, thou art my vassal.
    Away!
          [*Flings him off till he reels, almost to
               falling.*

De Tracy (lays hold of the pall). Come; as
    he said, thou art our prisoner.

Becket.   Down!
          [*Throws him headlong.*

Fitzurse (advances with drawn sword). I told
    thee that I should remember thee!

Becket. Profligate pander!

Fitzurse. Do you hear that? strike, strike!
        [*Strikes off the* ARCHBISHOP'S *mitre, and
          wounds him in the forehead.*

Becket (covers his eyes with his hand). I
    do commend my cause to God, the
    Virgin,
St. Denis of France and St. Alphege of
    England,
And all the tutelar Saints of Canterbury.
          [GRIM *wraps his arms about the* ARCH-
          BISHOP.
Spare this defence, dear brother.
          [TRACY *has arisen, and approaches,*
              hesitatingly, with his sword
              raised.
Fitzurse.   Strike him, Tracy!
Rosamund (rushing down steps from the choir).
    No, No, No, No!
Fitzurse. This wanton here. De Morville,
Hold her away.
De Morville. I hold her.
Rosamund (held back by DE MORVILLE, *and*
    stretching out her arms). Mercy, mercy,
As you would hope for mercy.
Fitzurse.   Strike, I say.
Grim. O God, O noble knights, O sacrilege!
Strike our Archbishop in his own cathedral!
The Pope, the King, will curse you—the whole
    world
Abhor you ; ye will die the death of dogs !
Nay, nay, good Tracy.   [*Lifts his arm.*
Fitzurse.   Answer not, but strike.

De Tracy. There is my answer then.

> [*Sword falls on* Grim's *arm, and glances from it, wounding* Becket.

Grim.   Mine arm is sever'd.
I can no more—fight out the good fight—
die
Conqueror.

> [*Staggers into the chapel of St. Benedict.*

Becket (*falling on his knees*). At the right
hand of Power—
Power and great glory—for thy Church, O
Lord—
Into Thy hands, O Lord—into Thy hands !—

> [*Sinks prone.*

De Brito. This last to rid thee of a world of
brawls !   [*Kills him.*
The traitor's dead, and will arise no more.

Fitzurse. Nay, have we still'd him ? What !
the great Archbishop !
Does he breathe ? No ?

De Tracy. No, Reginald, he is dead.

(*Storm bursts.*)*

De Morville. Will the earth gape and swallow
us ?

------

* *A tremendous thunderstorm actually broke over the Cathedral as the
murderers were leaving it.*

De Brito. The deed's done—
Away!

> [DE BRITO, DE TRACY, FITZURSE, *rush out,*
> *crying "King's men!"* DE MORVILLE *fol-*
> *lows slowly. Flashes of lightning thro' the*
> *Cathedral.* ROSAMUND *seen kneeling by the*
> *body of* BECKET.